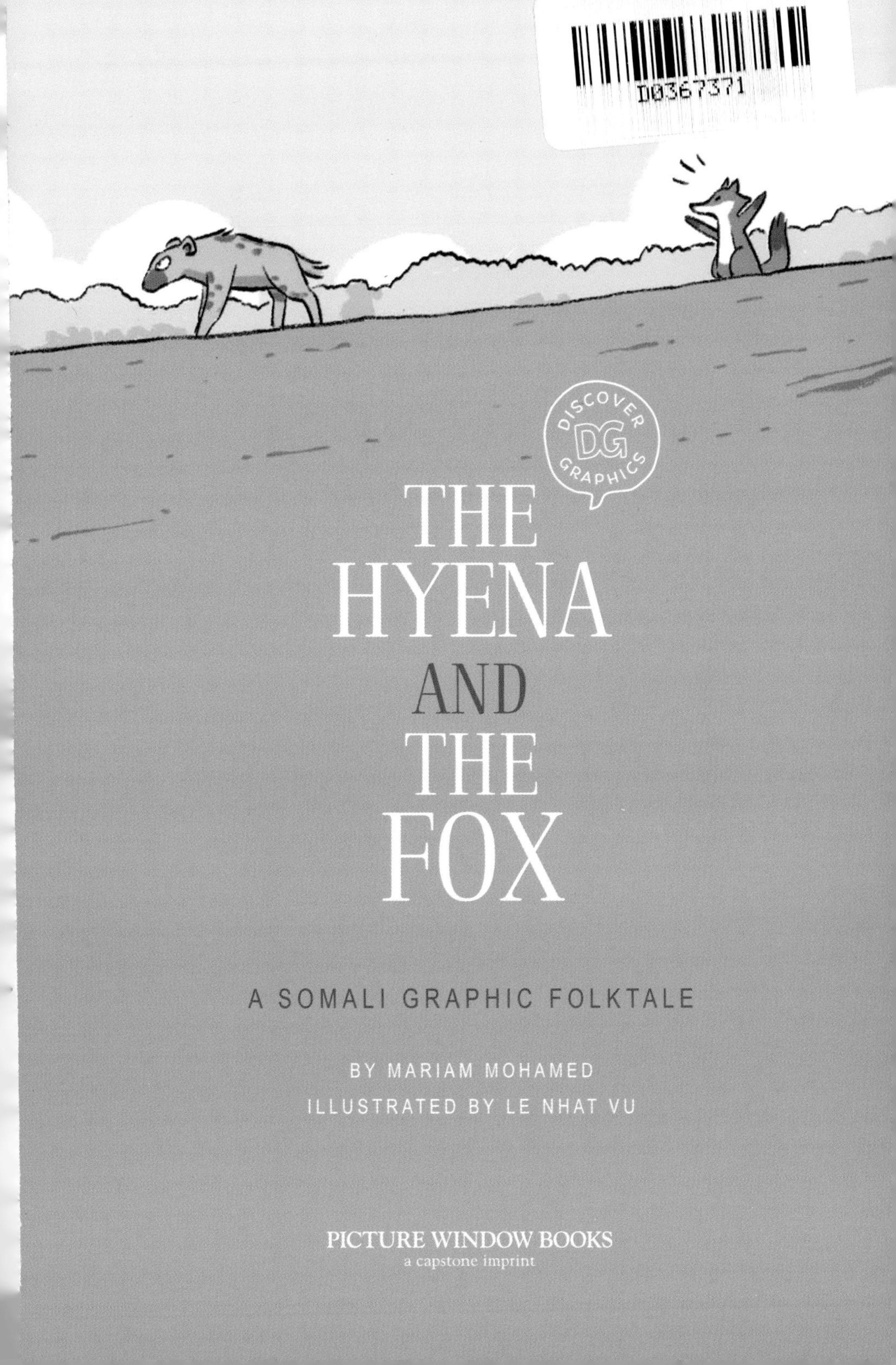

DISCOVER GRAPHICS

THE HYENA AND THE FOX

A SOMALI GRAPHIC FOLKTALE

BY MARIAM MOHAMED
ILLUSTRATED BY LE NHAT VU

PICTURE WINDOW BOOKS
a capstone imprint

Published by Picture Window Books, an imprint of Capstone
1710 Roe Crest Drive, North Mankato, Minnesota 56003
capstonepub.com

Library of Congress Cataloging-in-Publication Data is available on the Library of Congress website.

ISBN: 9781484672662 (hardcover)
ISBN: 9781484672617 (paperback)
ISBN: 9781484672624 (ebook PDF)

Summary: When a fox keeps eating a farmer's animals, the farmer, his wife, and a few herdsmen come up with a plan to get rid of the problem. But the clever fox has other ideas and gets some help from a hyena.

Editorial Credits
Editor: Ericka Smith; Designer: Kay Fraser; Production Specialist: Katy LaVigne

Author's Note

Thank you so much for reading *The Hyena and the Fox.* I hope you enjoy reading this story and learn from Fox's and Hyena's mistakes.

I grew up hearing this popular Somali folktale, and now I share it with my two daughters. Maybe they'll share it with their kids one day too.

To my girls, Faduma and Kinsi, this book is dedicated to you.

Love you!

Hooyo

Printed and bound in the USA. 5195

CAST OF CHARACTERS

Fox is very sneaky and clever.

Hyena is greedy and falls for tricks easily.

Asha is married to Farmer Ahmed. She is angry with Fox and wants to trap her.

Farmer Ahmed is married to Asha. He is upset with Fox and wants to trap her too.

The **herdsmen** want to help Asha and Farmer Ahmed.

HOW TO READ A GRAPHIC NOVEL

Graphic novels are easy to read. Boxes called panels show you how to follow the story. Look at the panels from left to right and top to bottom.

Read the word boxes and word balloons from left to right as well. Don't forget the sound and action words in the pictures.

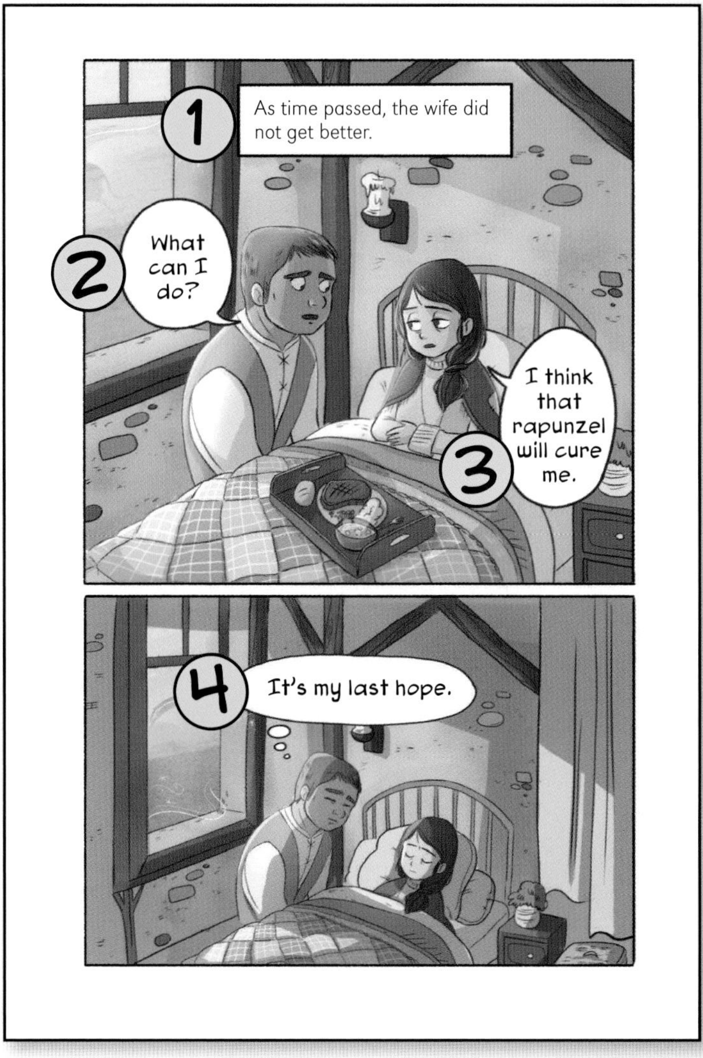
1
As time passed, the wife did not get better.
2
What can I do?
3
I think that rapunzel will cure me.
4
It's my last hope.

The pictures and the words work together to tell the whole story.

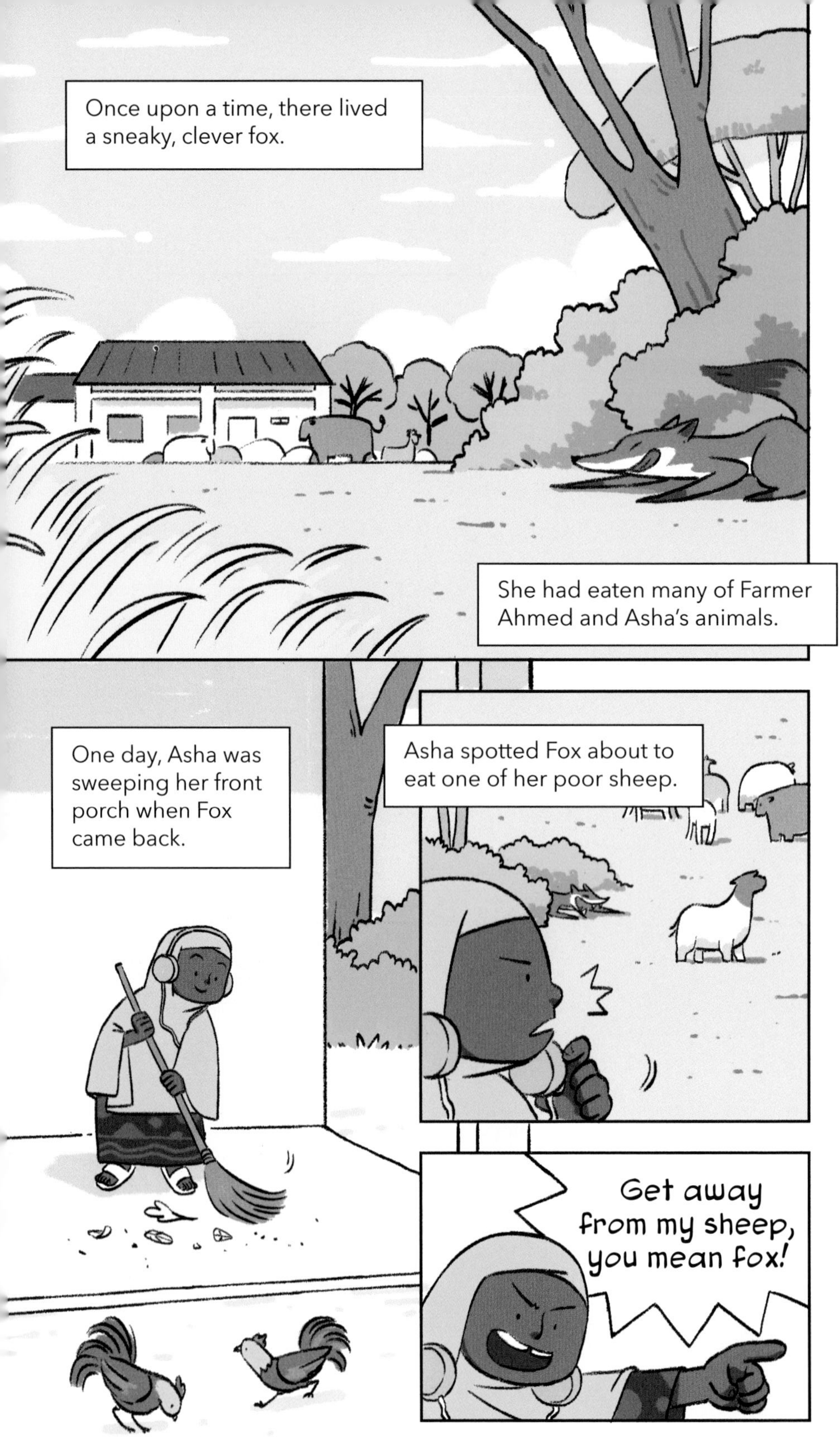
Once upon a time, there lived a sneaky, clever fox.
She had eaten many of Farmer Ahmed and Asha's animals.
One day, Asha was sweeping her front porch when Fox came back.
Asha spotted Fox about to eat one of her poor sheep.
Get away from my sheep, you mean fox!

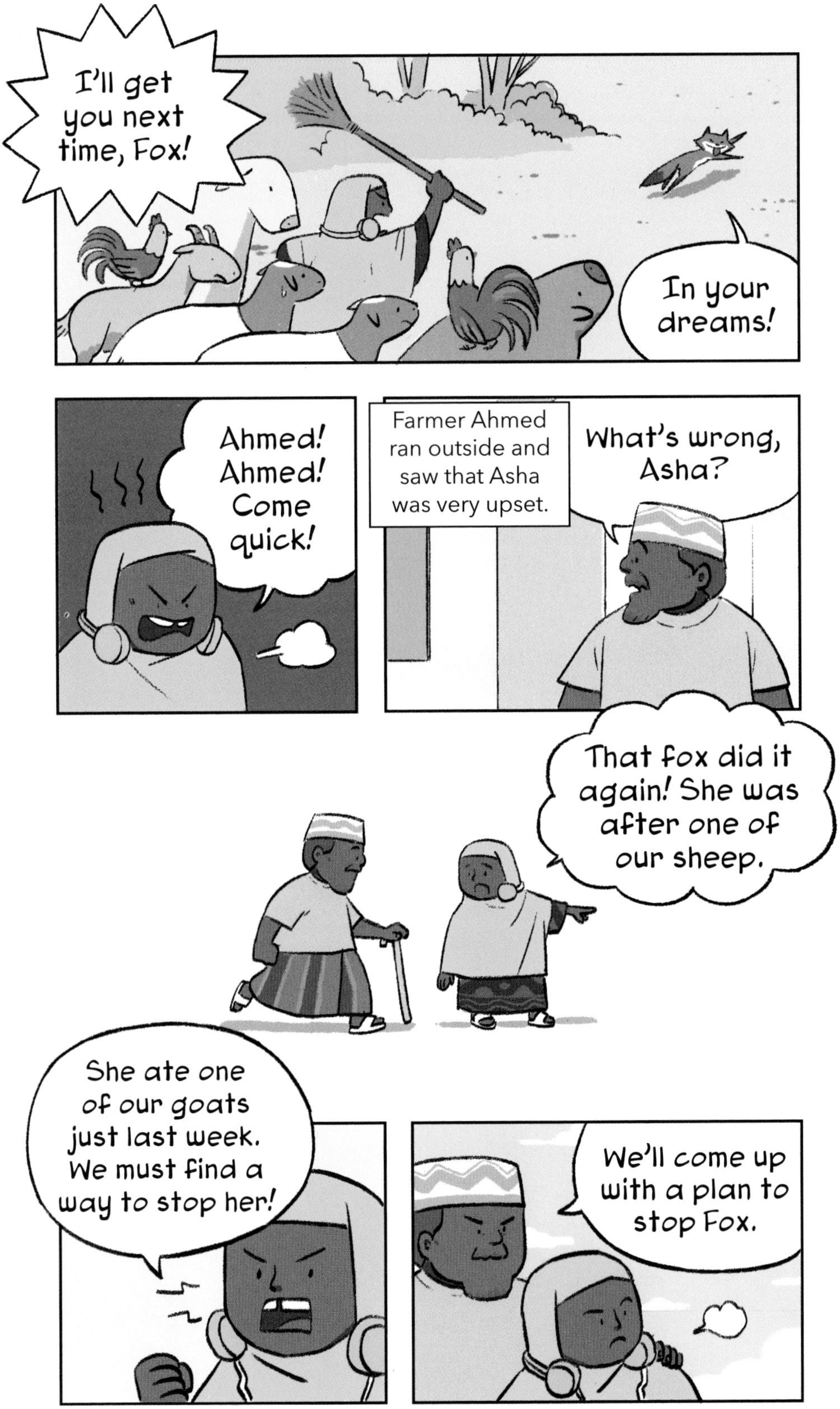

I'll get you next time, Fox!
In your dreams!
Ahmed! Ahmed! Come quick!
Farmer Ahmed ran outside and saw that Asha was very upset.
What's wrong, Asha?
That fox did it again! She was after one of our sheep.
She ate one of our goats just last week. We must find a way to stop her!
We'll come up with a plan to stop Fox.

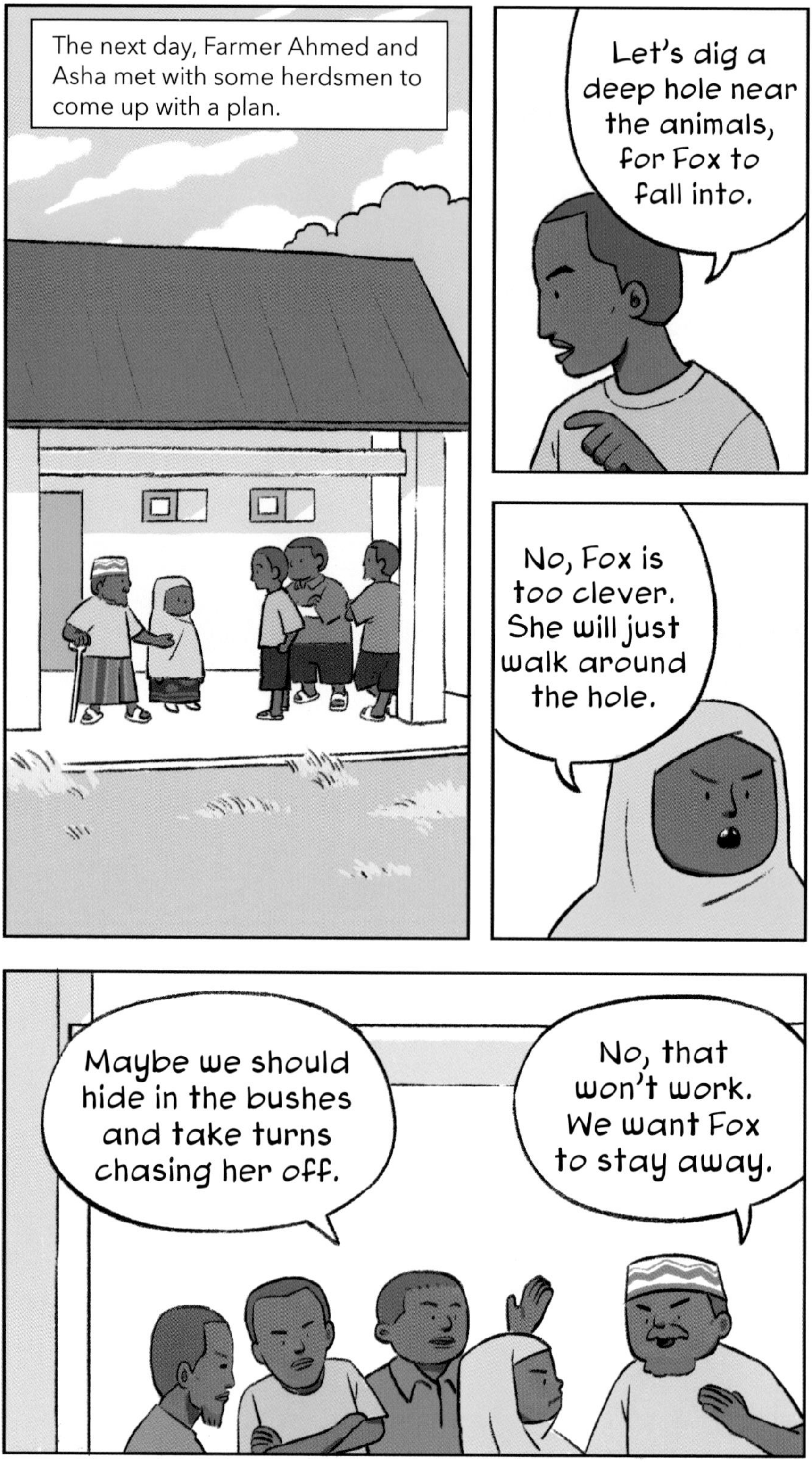
The next day, Farmer Ahmed and Asha met with some herdsmen to come up with a plan.
Let's dig a deep hole near the animals, for Fox to fall into.
No, Fox is too clever. She will just walk around the hole.
Maybe we should hide in the bushes and take turns chasing her off.
No, that won't work. We want Fox to stay away.

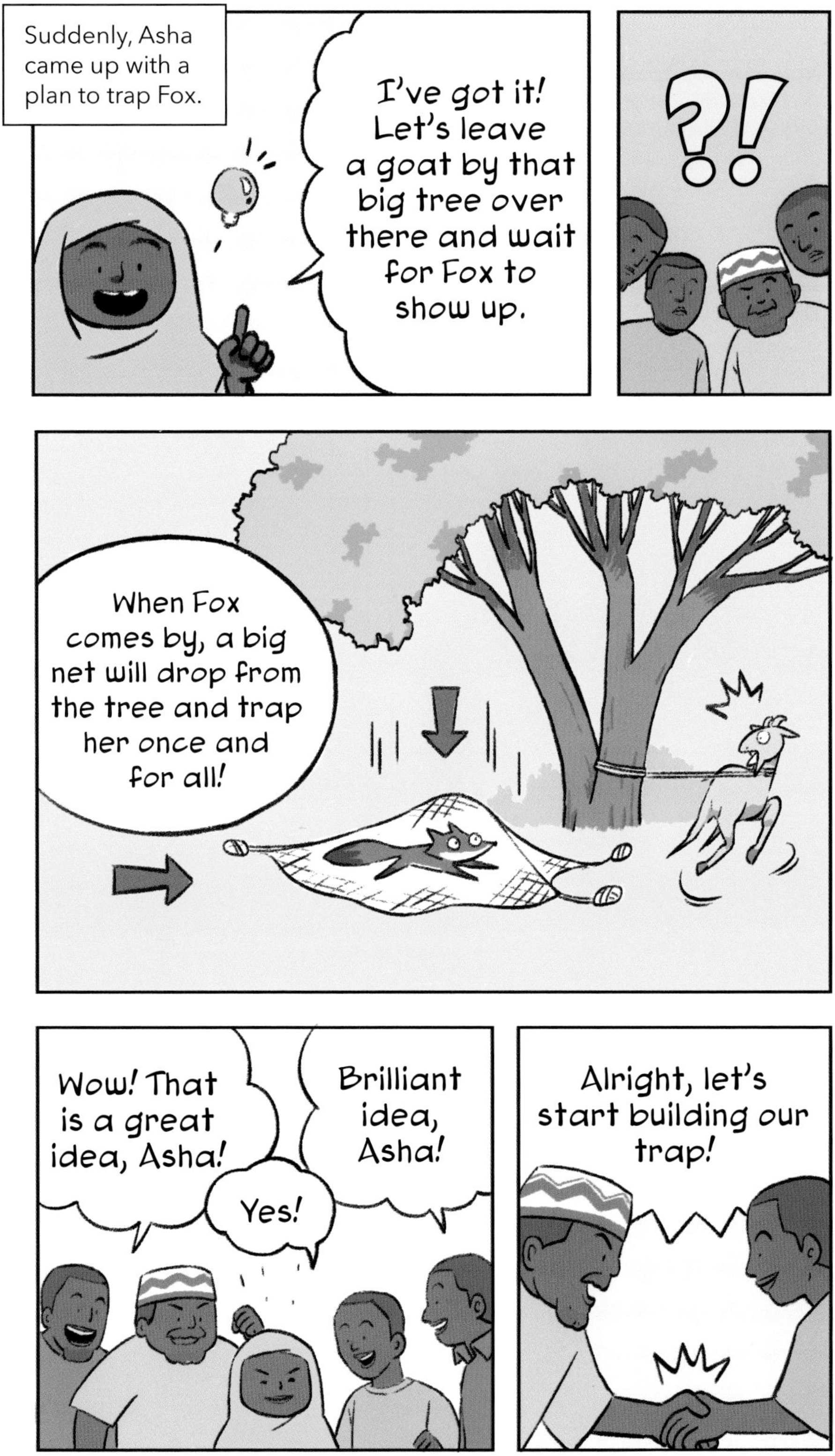
Suddenly, Asha came up with a plan to trap Fox.
I've got it! Let's leave a goat by that big tree over there and wait for Fox to show up.
?!
When Fox comes by, a big net will drop from the tree and trap her once and for all!
Wow! That is a great idea, Asha!
Yes!
Brilliant idea, Asha!
Alright, let's start building our trap!

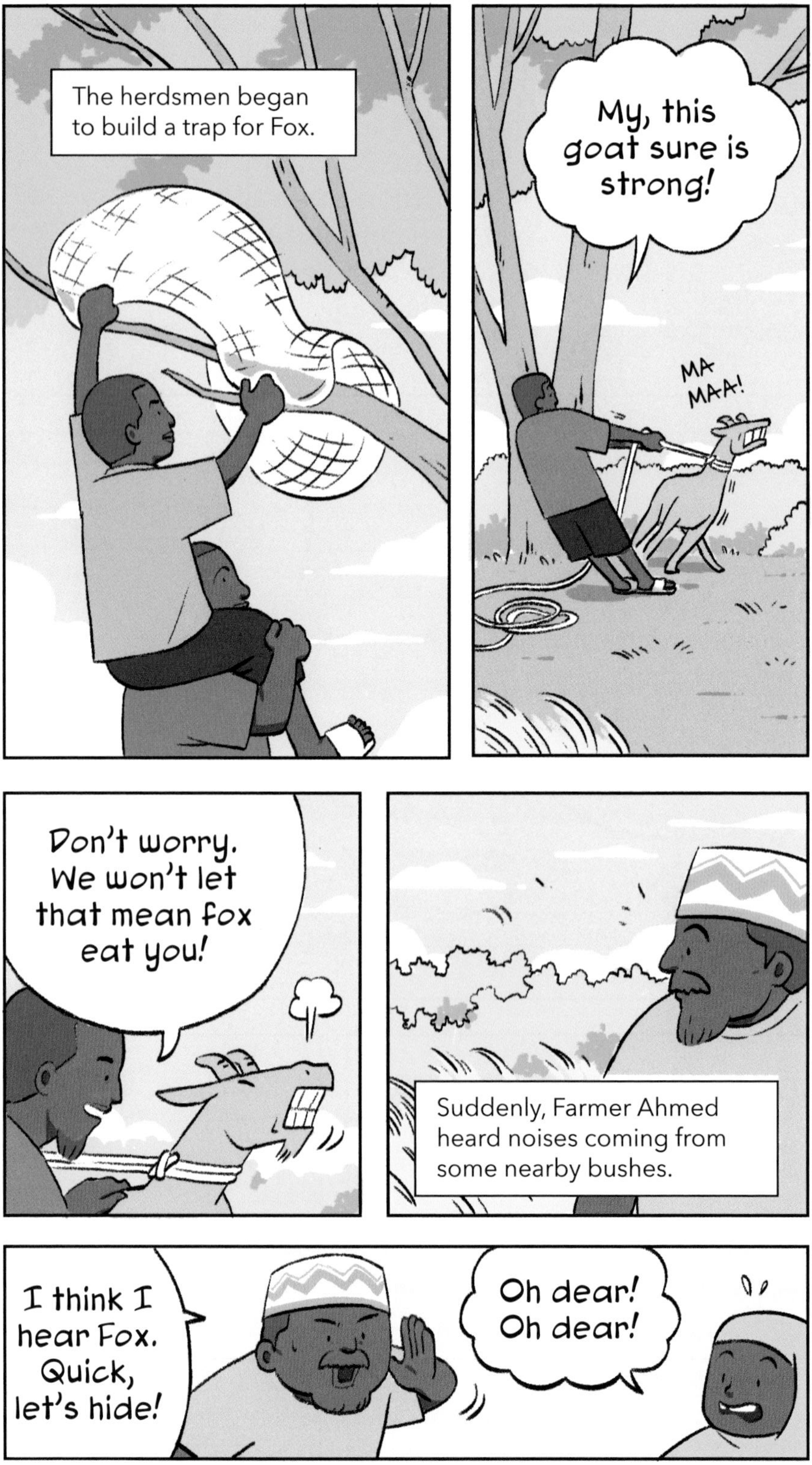
The herdsmen began to build a trap for Fox.
My, this goat sure is strong!
MA MAA!
Don't worry. We won't let that mean fox eat you!
Suddenly, Farmer Ahmed heard noises coming from some nearby bushes.
I think I hear Fox. Quick, let's hide!
Oh dear! Oh dear!

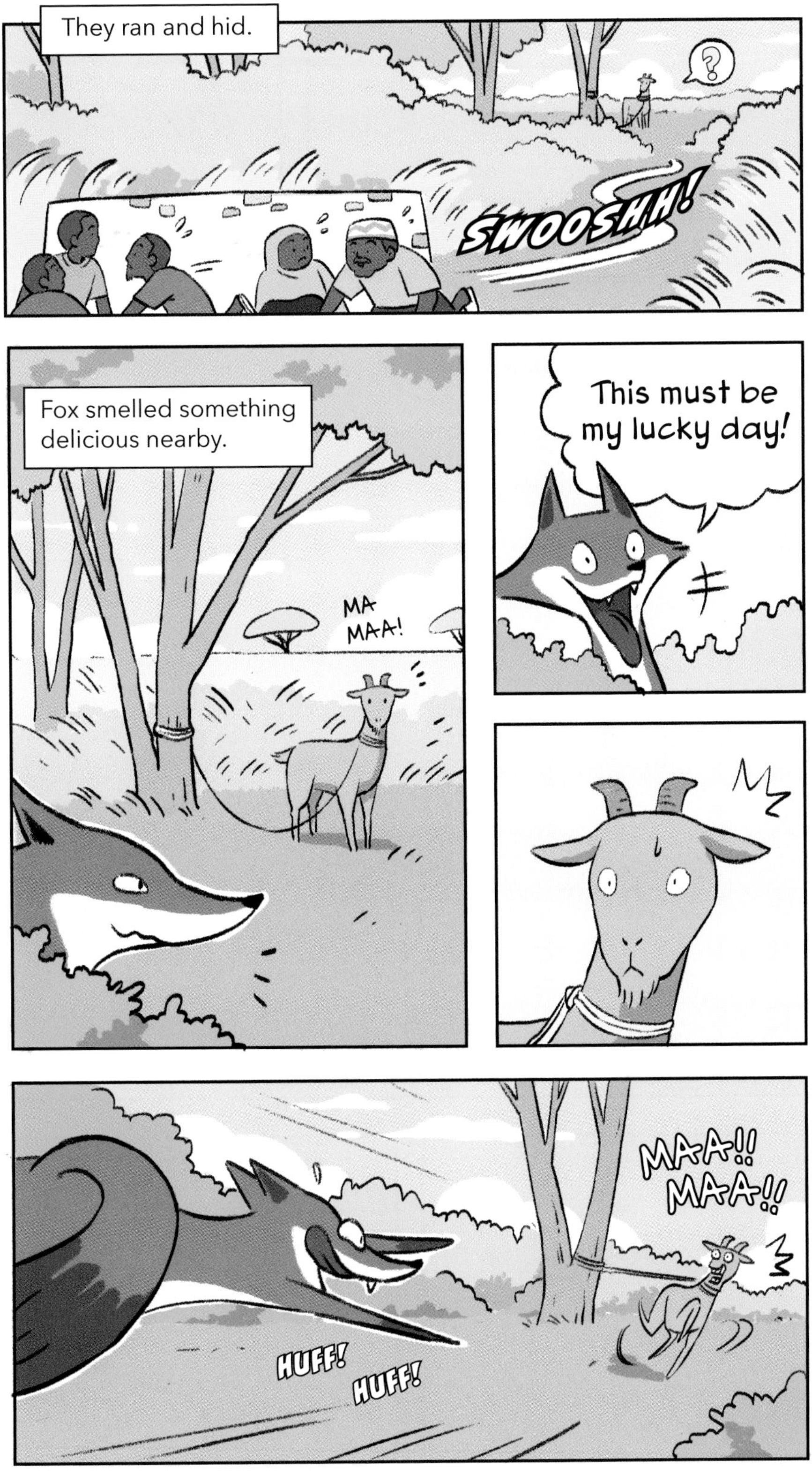
They ran and hid.
?
SWOOSHH!
Fox smelled something delicious nearby.
MA MAA!
This must be my lucky day!
MAA!! MAA!!
HUFF! HUFF!

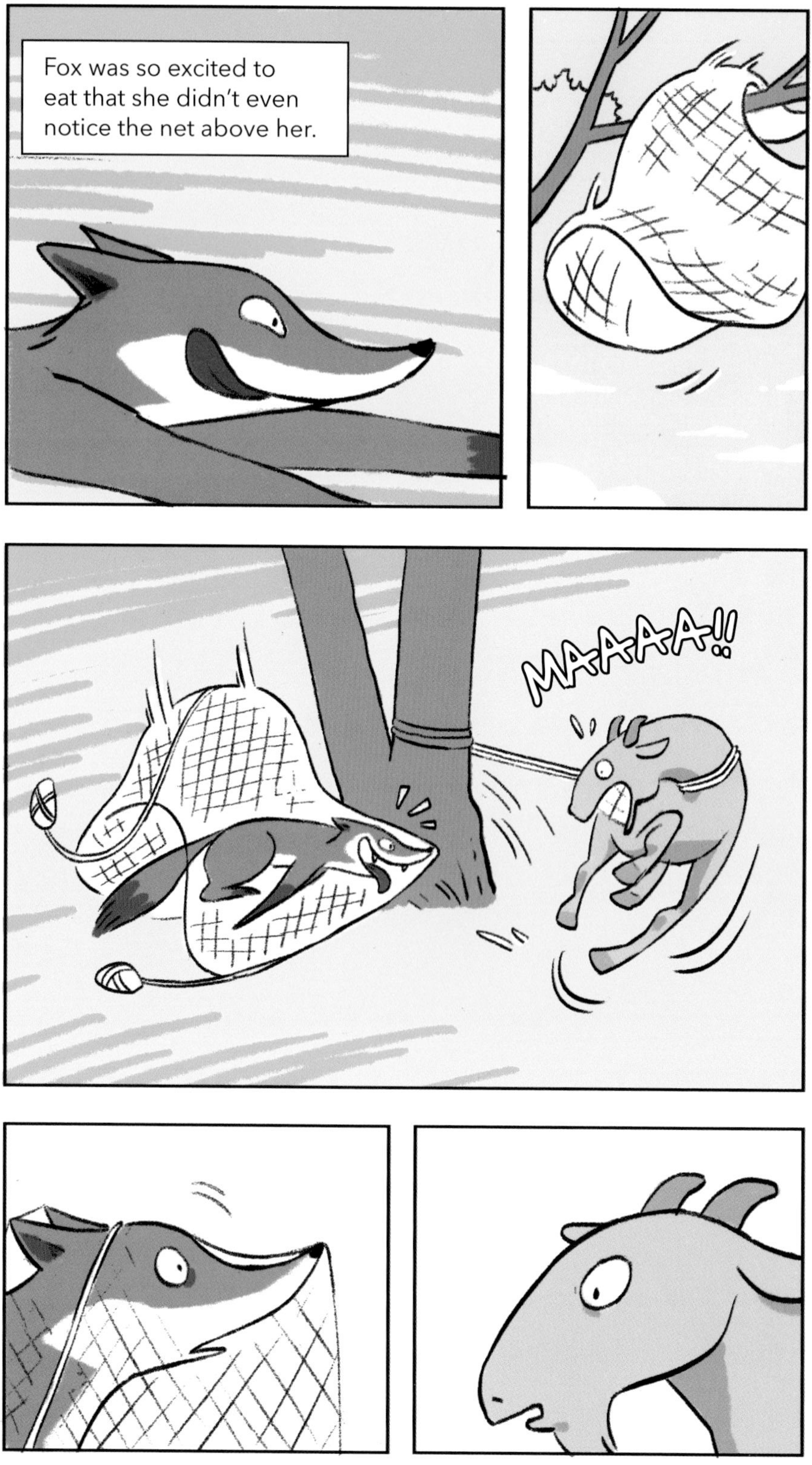
Fox was so excited to eat that she didn't even notice the net above her.
MAAAA!!

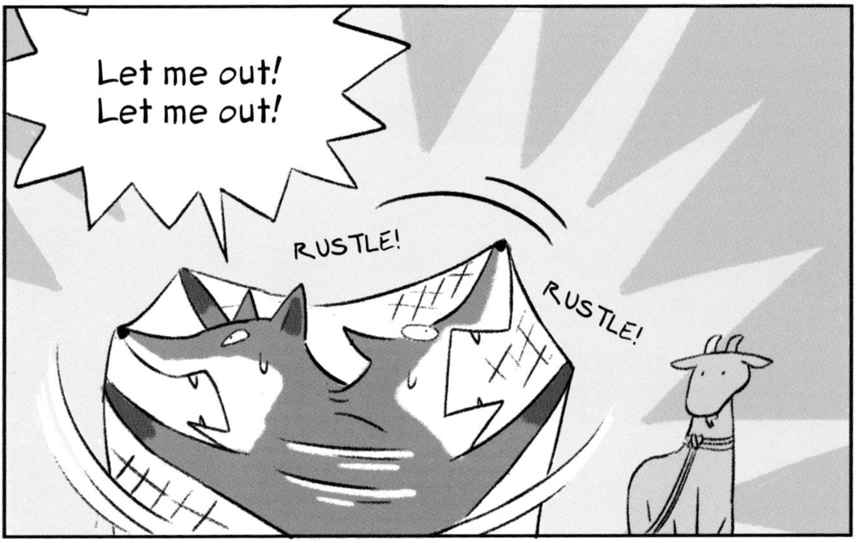
Let me out!
Let me out!
RUSTLE!
RUSTLE!

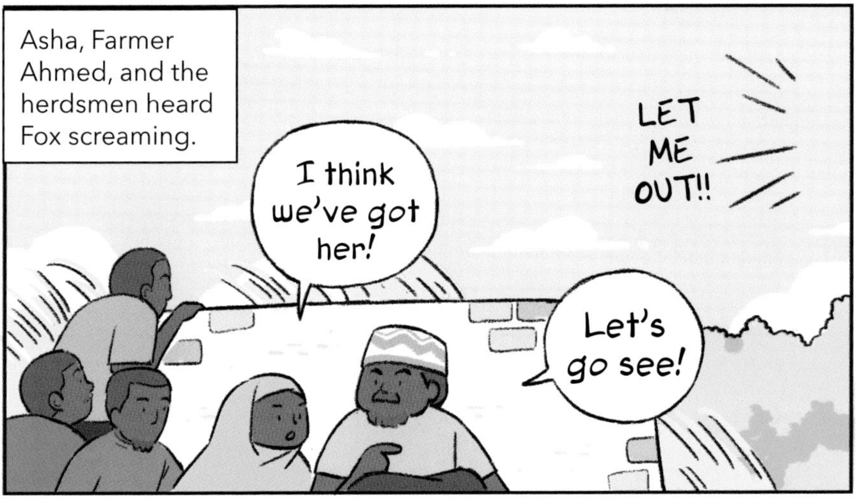
Asha, Farmer Ahmed, and the herdsmen heard Fox screaming.
I think we've got her!
LET ME OUT!!
Let's go see!

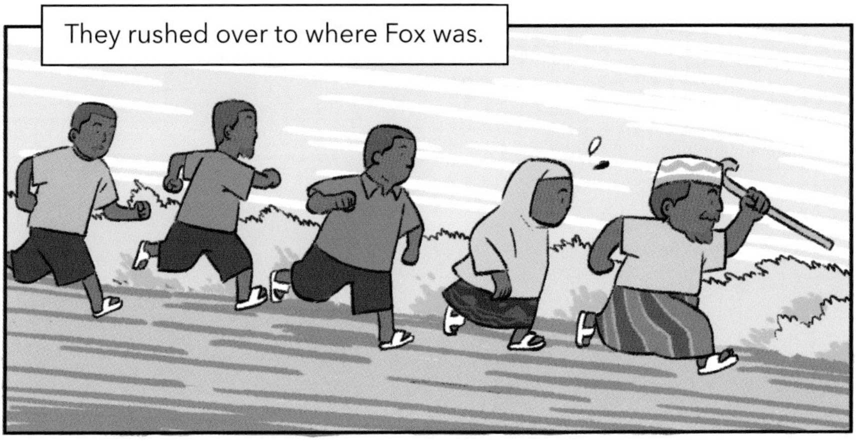
They rushed over to where Fox was.

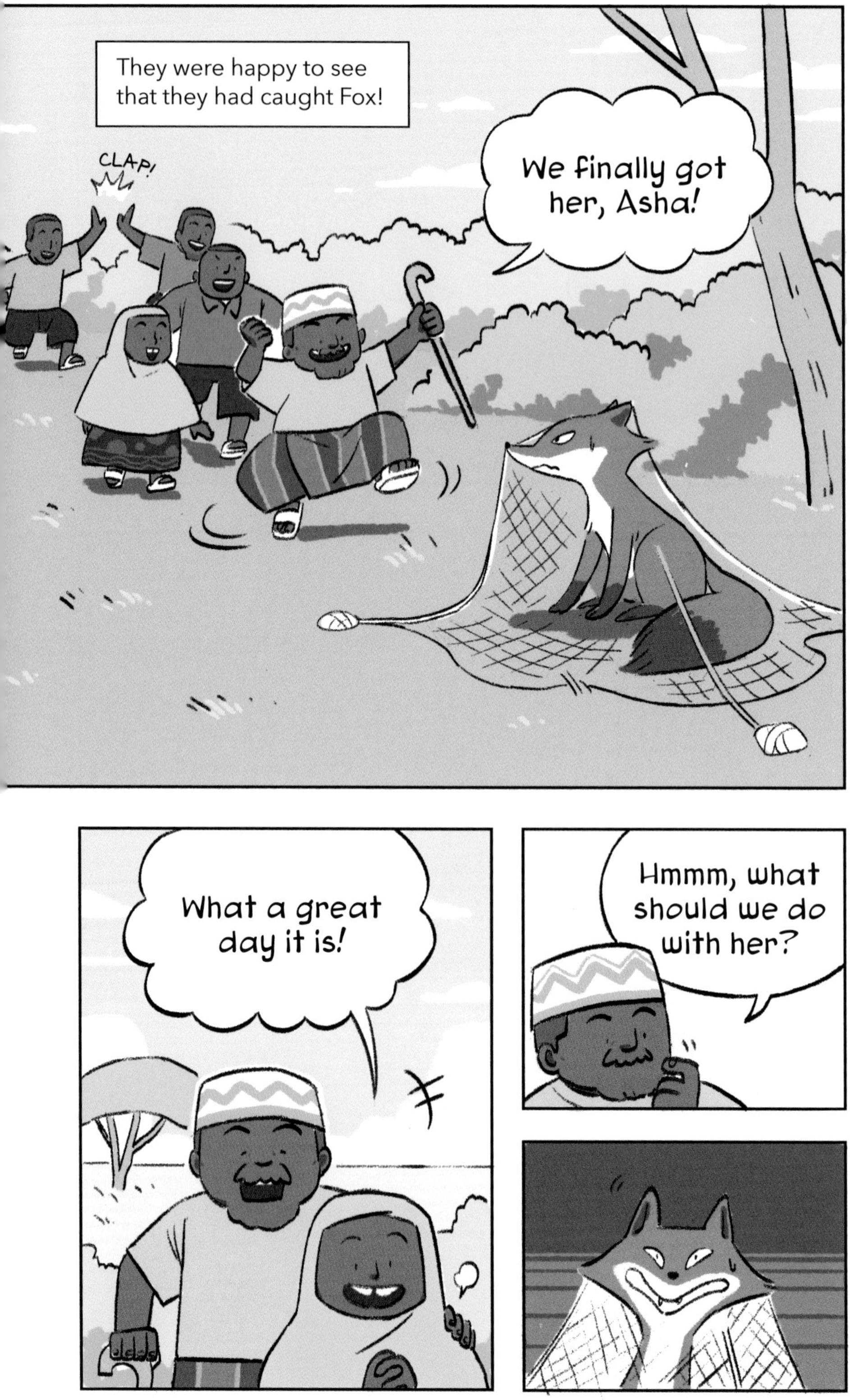
They were happy to see that they had caught Fox!
CLAP!
We finally got her, Asha!
What a great day it is!
Hmmm, what should we do with her?

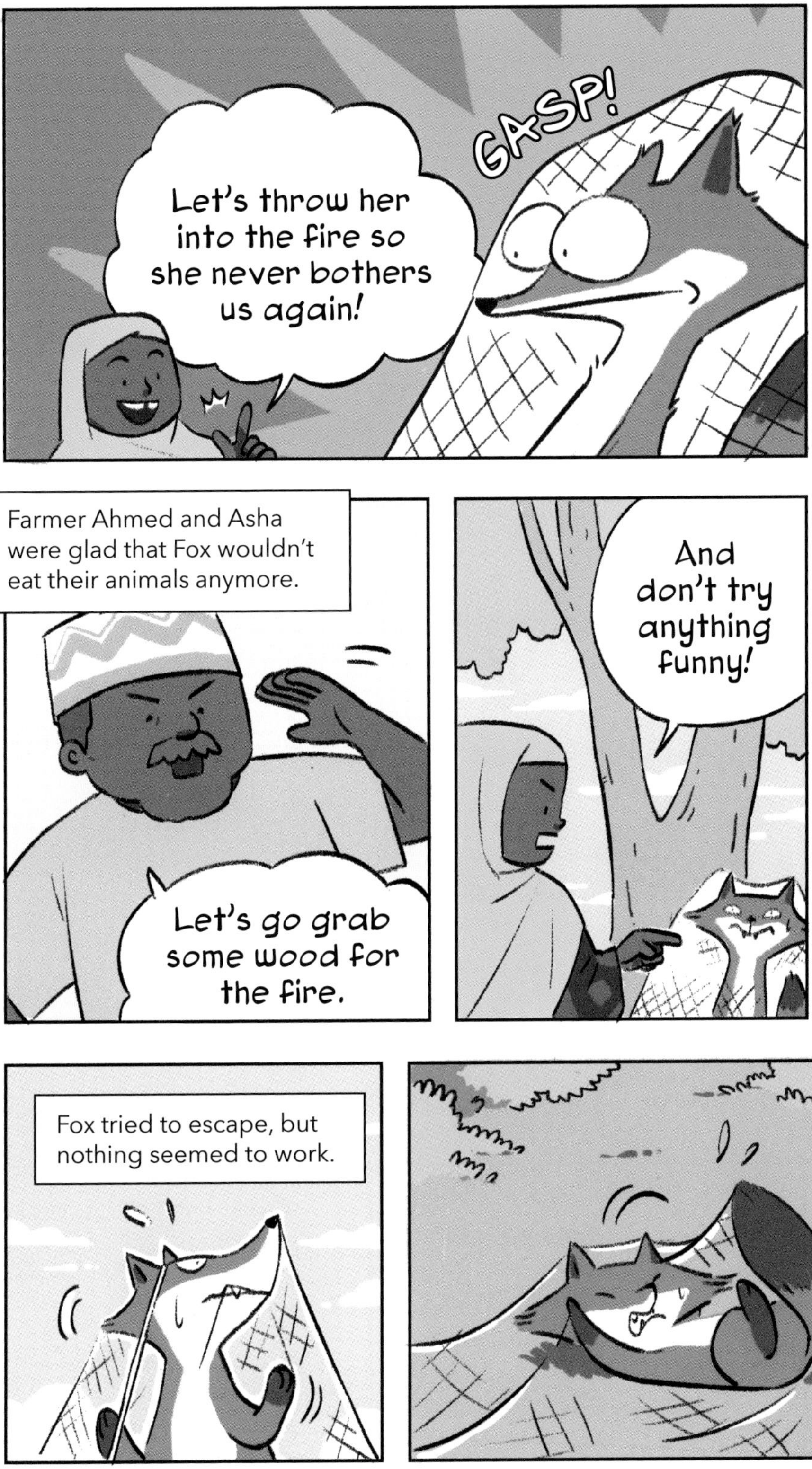
Let's throw her into the fire so she never bothers us again!
GASP!
Farmer Ahmed and Asha were glad that Fox wouldn't eat their animals anymore.
Let's go grab some wood for the fire.
And don't try anything funny!
Fox tried to escape, but nothing seemed to work.

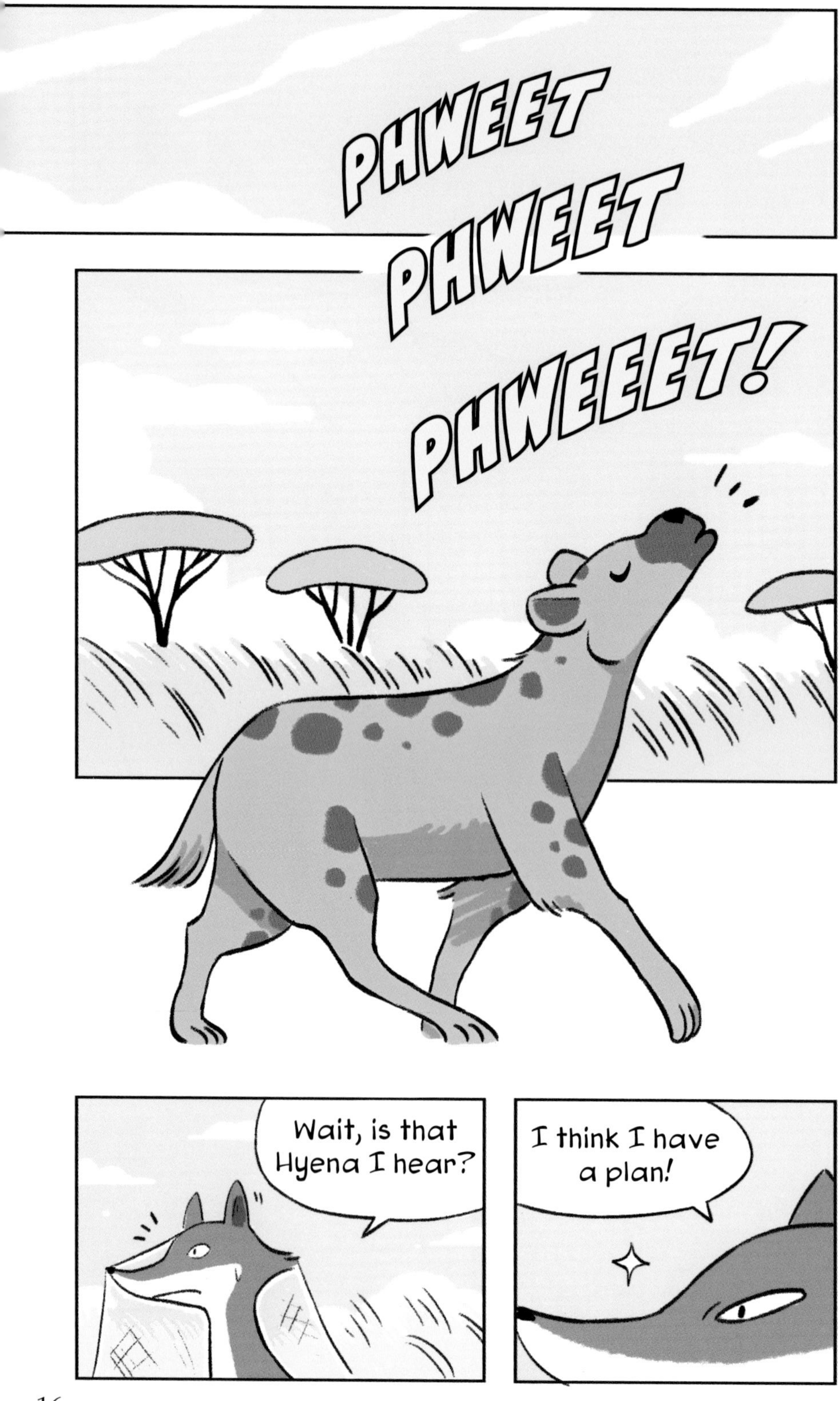
PHWEET
PHWEET
PHWEEET!
Wait, is that Hyena I hear?
I think I have a plan!

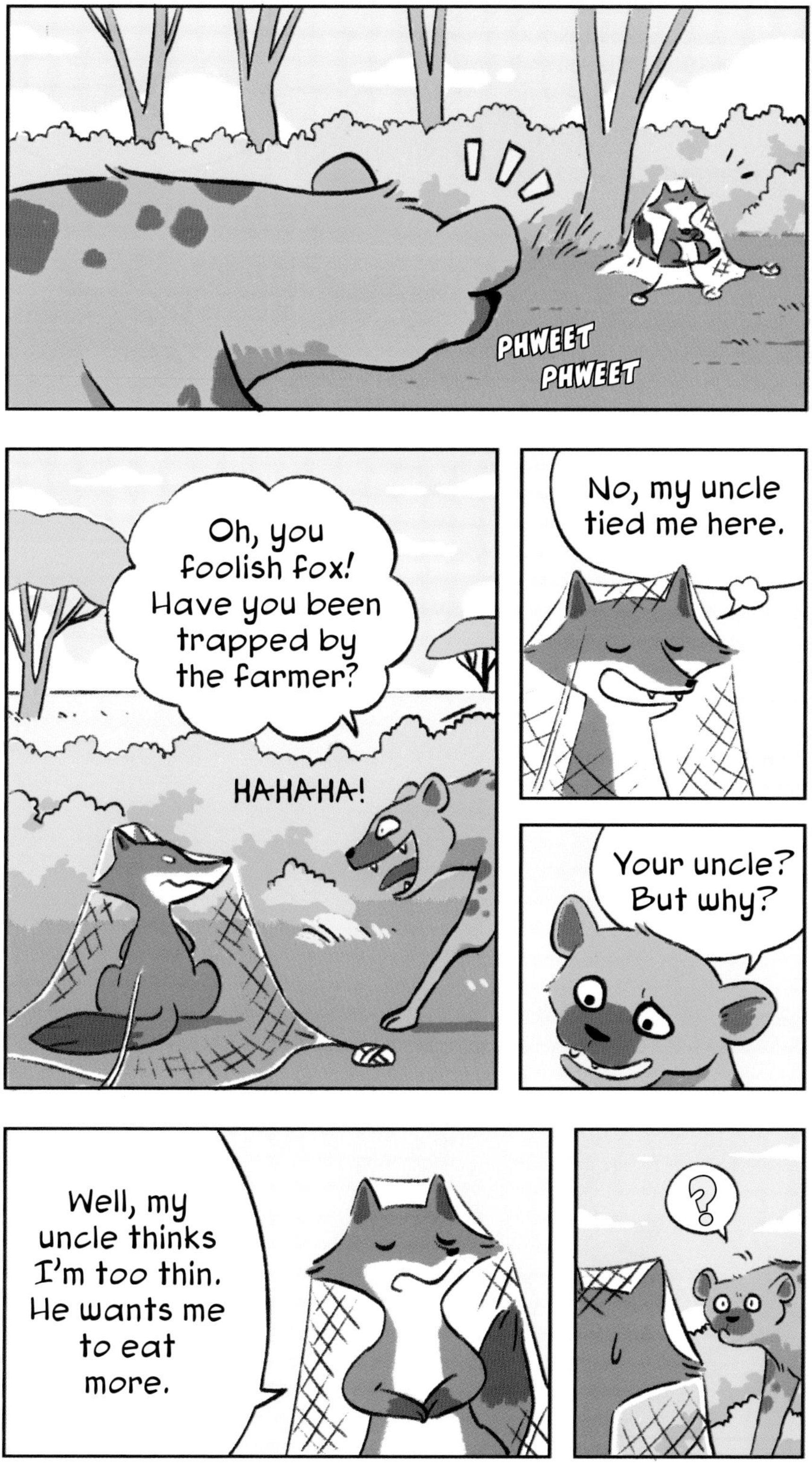
PHWEET
PHWEET
Oh, you foolish fox! Have you been trapped by the farmer?
HAHAHA!
No, my uncle tied me here.
Your uncle? But why?
Well, my uncle thinks I'm too thin. He wants me to eat more.
?

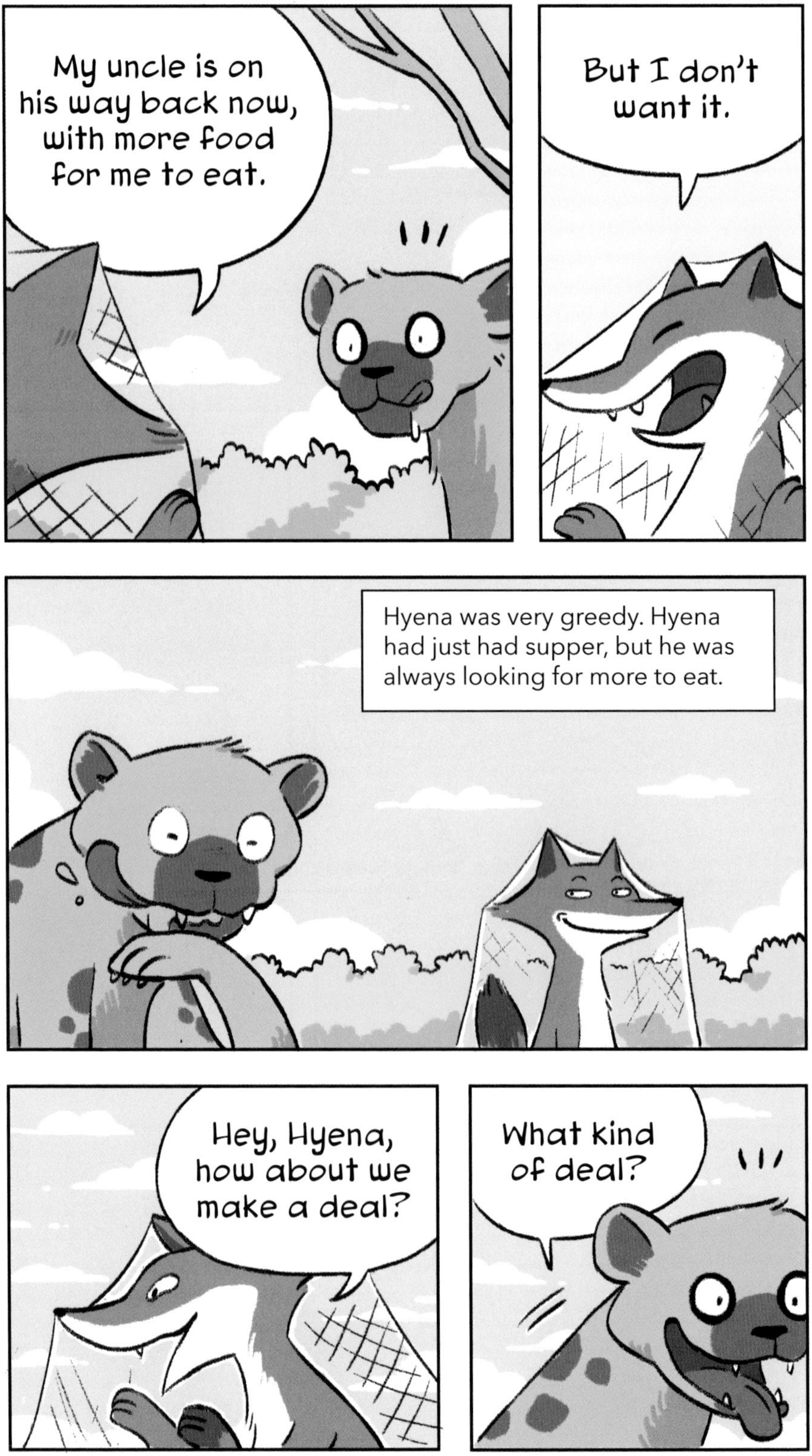
My uncle is on his way back now, with more food for me to eat.
But I don't want it.
Hyena was very greedy. Hyena had just had supper, but he was always looking for more to eat.
Hey, Hyena, how about we make a deal?
What kind of deal?

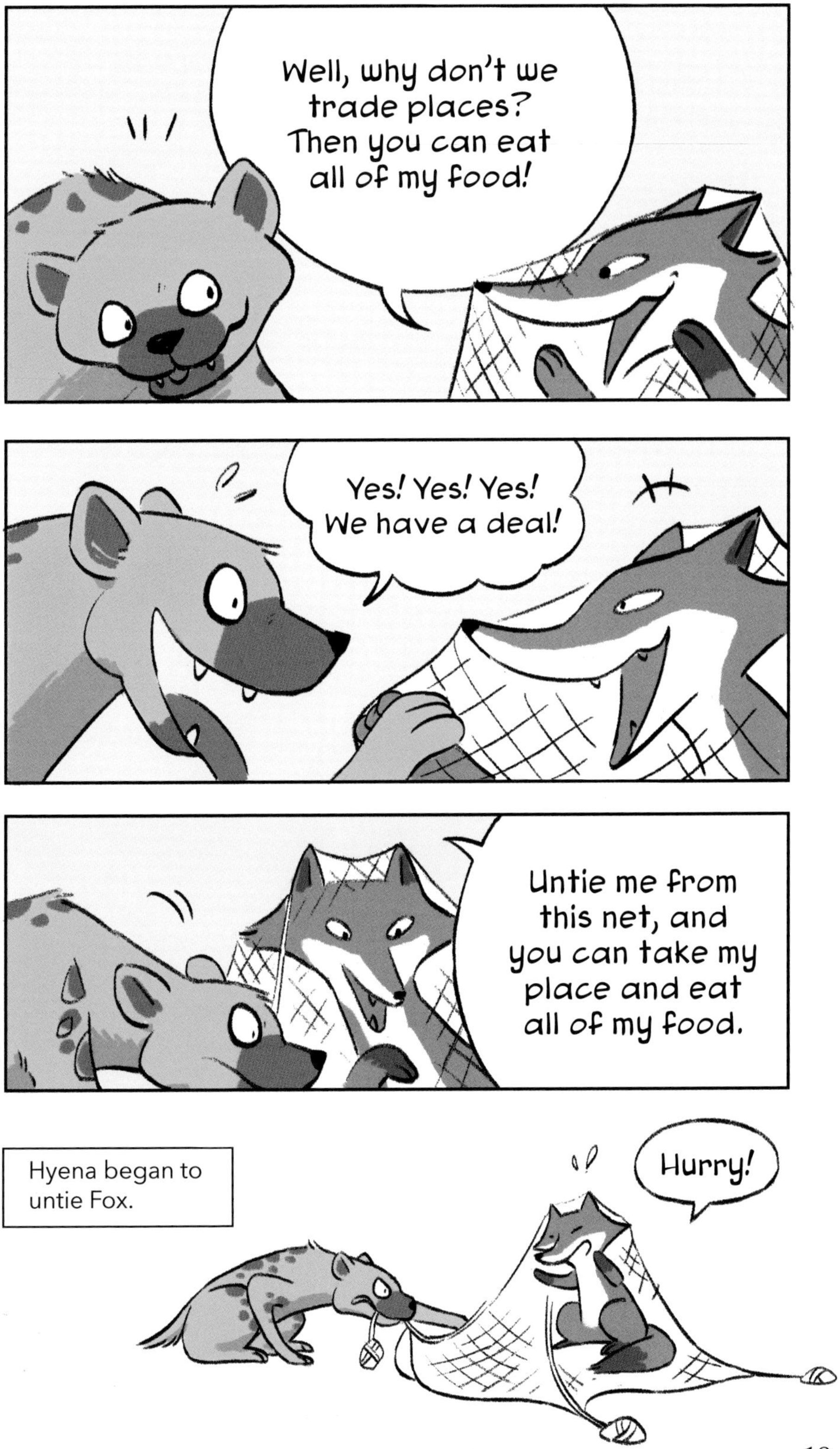
Well, why don't we trade places? Then you can eat all of my food!
Yes! Yes! Yes! We have a deal!
Untie me from this net, and you can take my place and eat all of my food.
Hyena began to untie Fox.
Hurry!

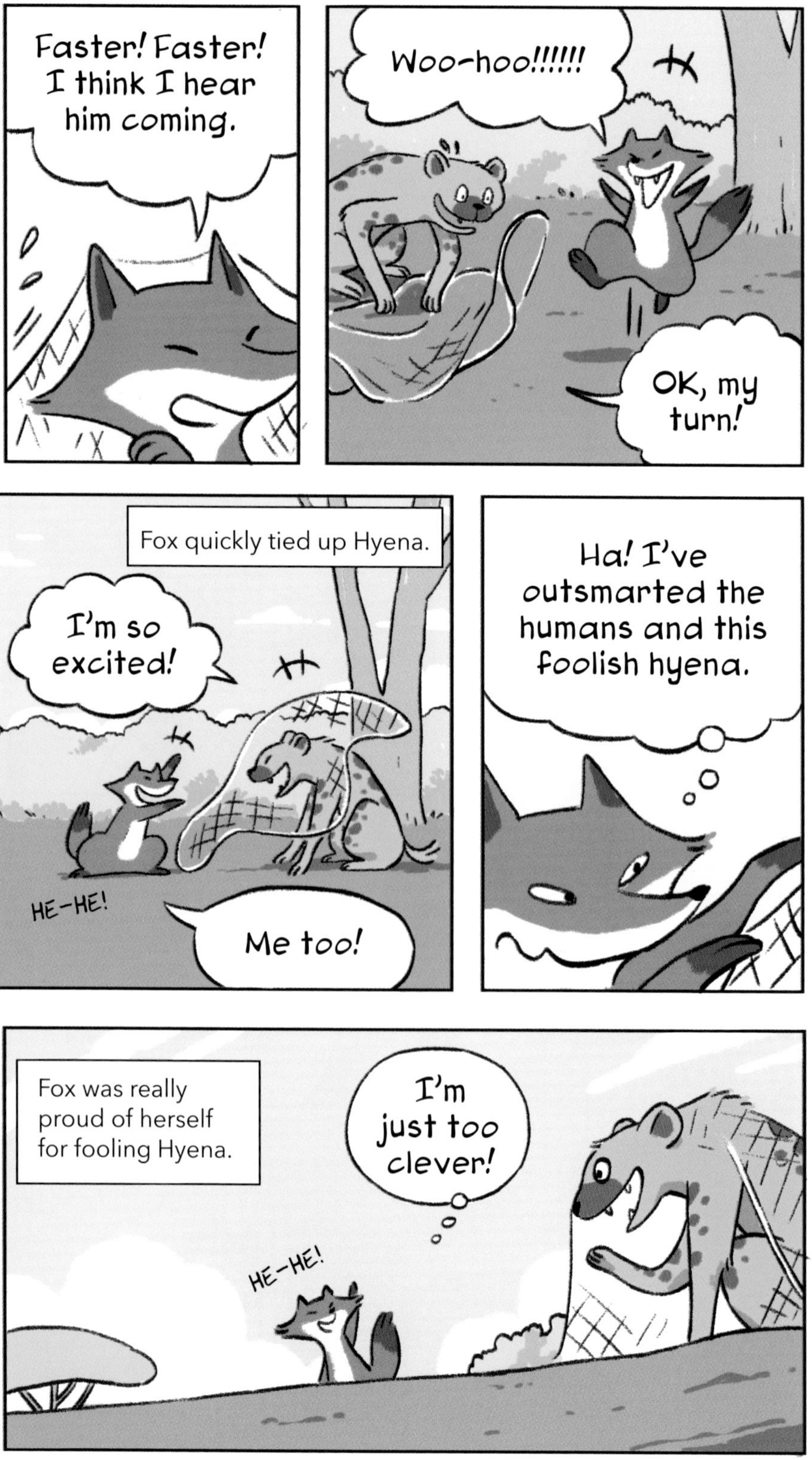
Faster! Faster! I think I hear him coming.
Woo-hoo!!!!!!
OK, my turn!
Fox quickly tied up Hyena.
I'm so excited!
HE-HE!
Me too!
Ha! I've outsmarted the humans and this foolish hyena.
Fox was really proud of herself for fooling Hyena.
I'm just too clever!
HE-HE!

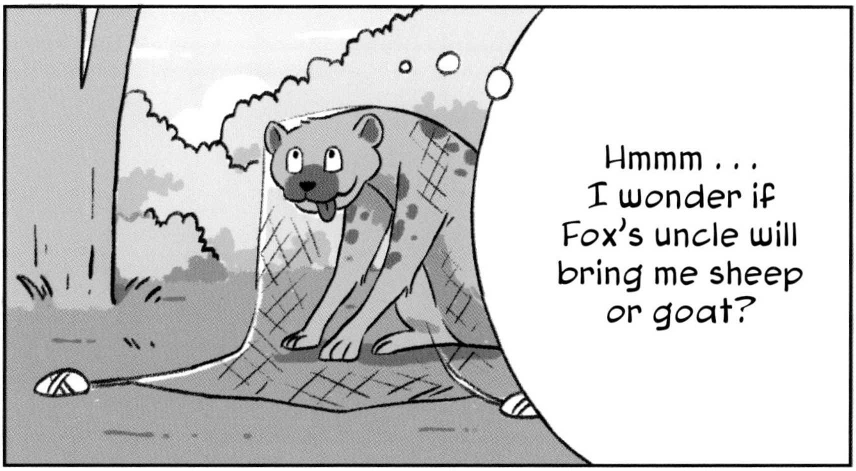
Hmmm . . . I wonder if Fox's uncle will bring me sheep or goat?

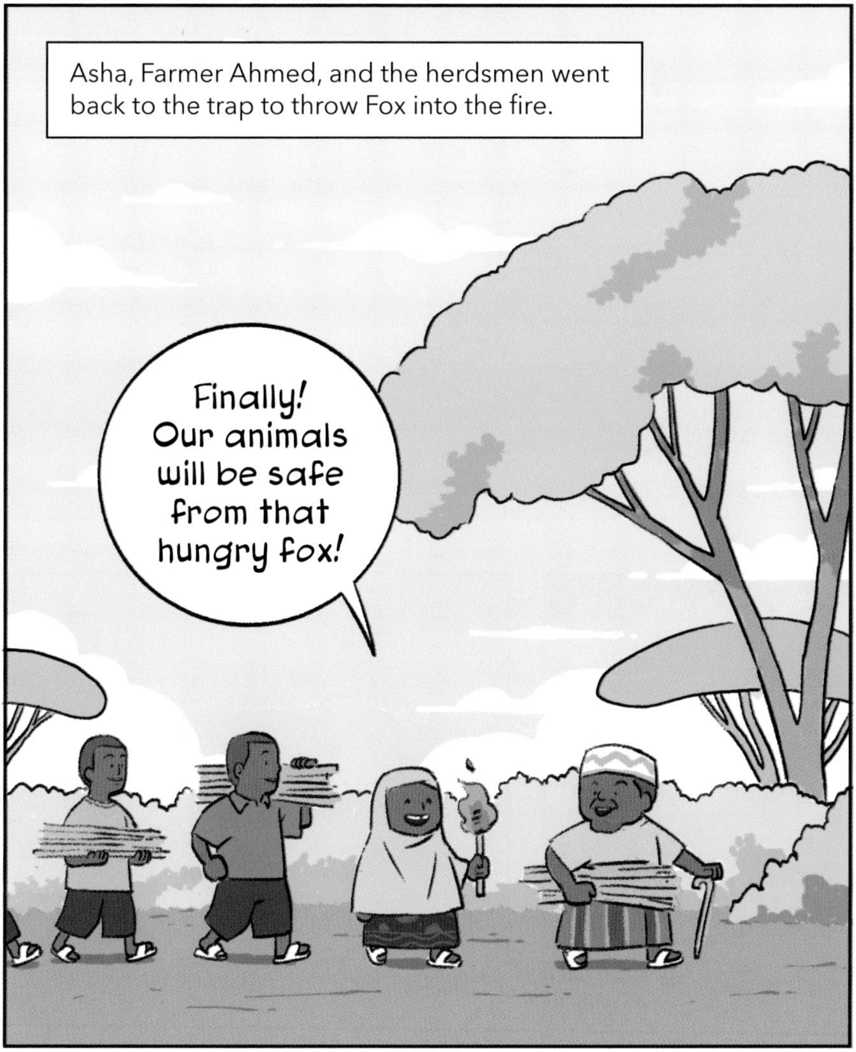
Asha, Farmer Ahmed, and the herdsmen went back to the trap to throw Fox into the fire.
Finally! Our animals will be safe from that hungry fox!

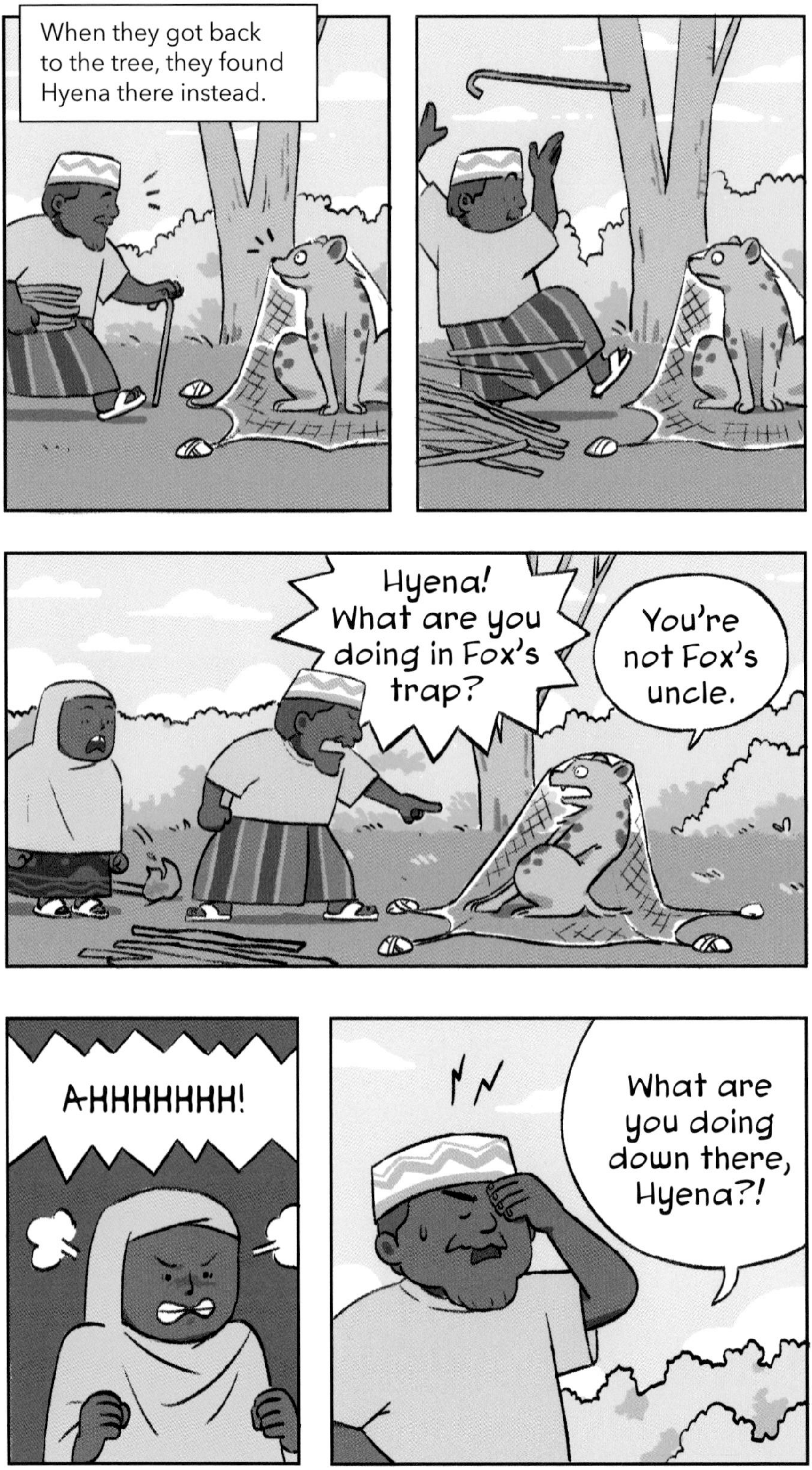
When they got back to the tree, they found Hyena there instead.
Hyena! What are you doing in Fox's trap?
You're not Fox's uncle.
AHHHHHHH!
What are you doing down there, Hyena?!

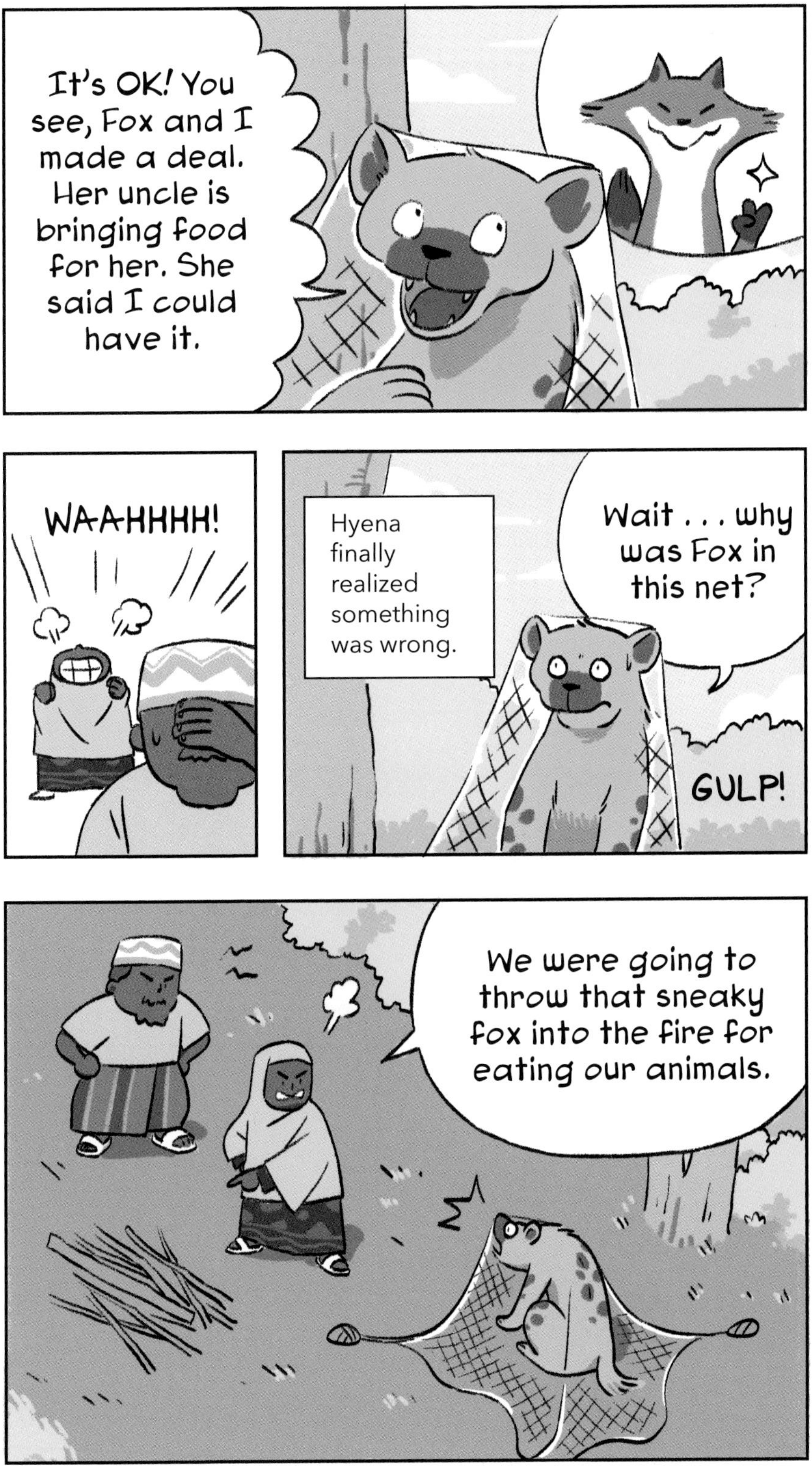
It's OK! You see, Fox and I made a deal. Her uncle is bringing food for her. She said I could have it.
WAAHHHH!
Hyena finally realized something was wrong.
Wait . . . why was Fox in this net?
GULP!
We were going to throw that sneaky fox into the fire for eating our animals.

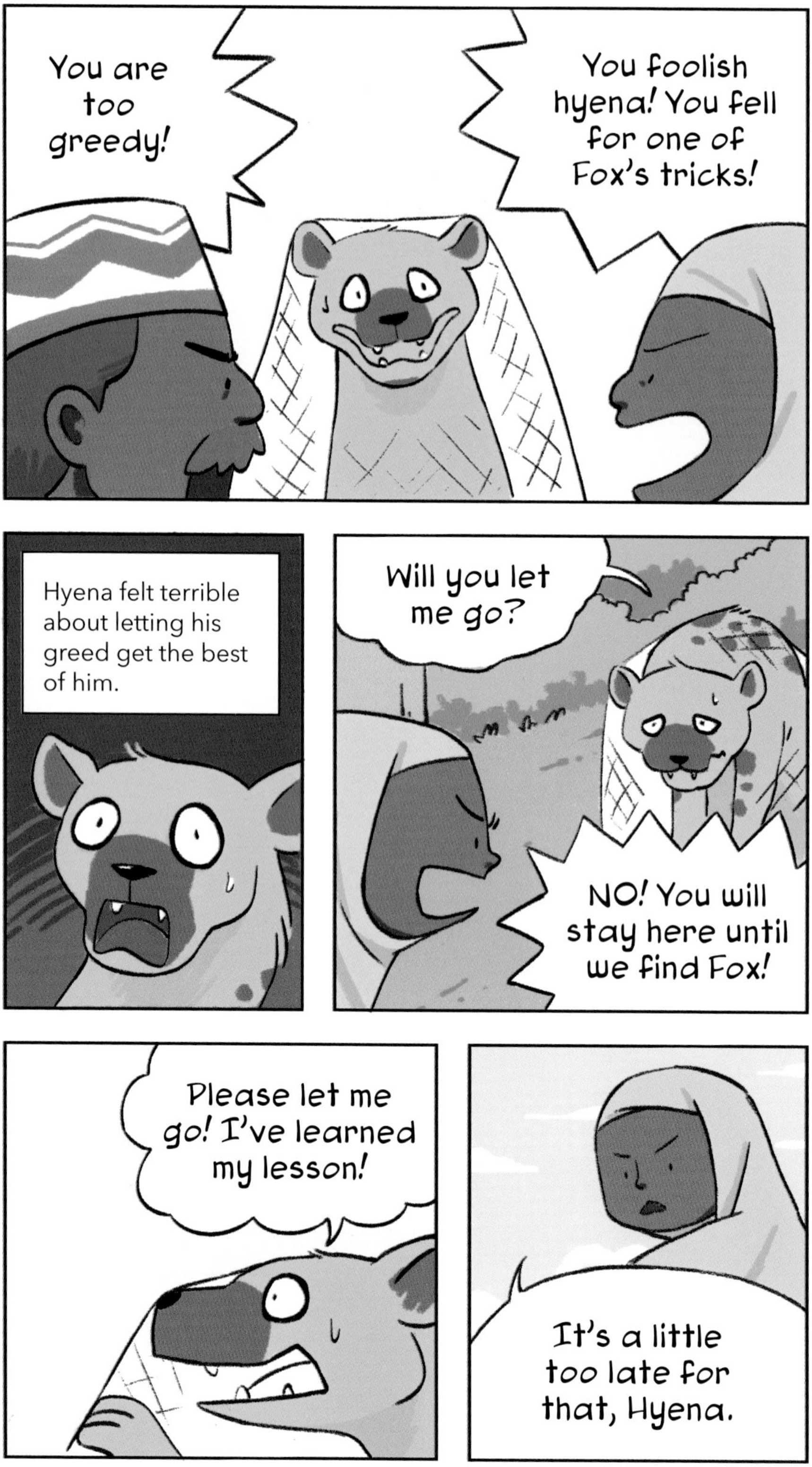
You are too greedy!
You foolish hyena! You fell for one of Fox's tricks!
Hyena felt terrible about letting his greed get the best of him.
Will you let me go?
NO! You will stay here until we find Fox!
Please let me go! I've learned my lesson!
It's a little too late for that, Hyena.

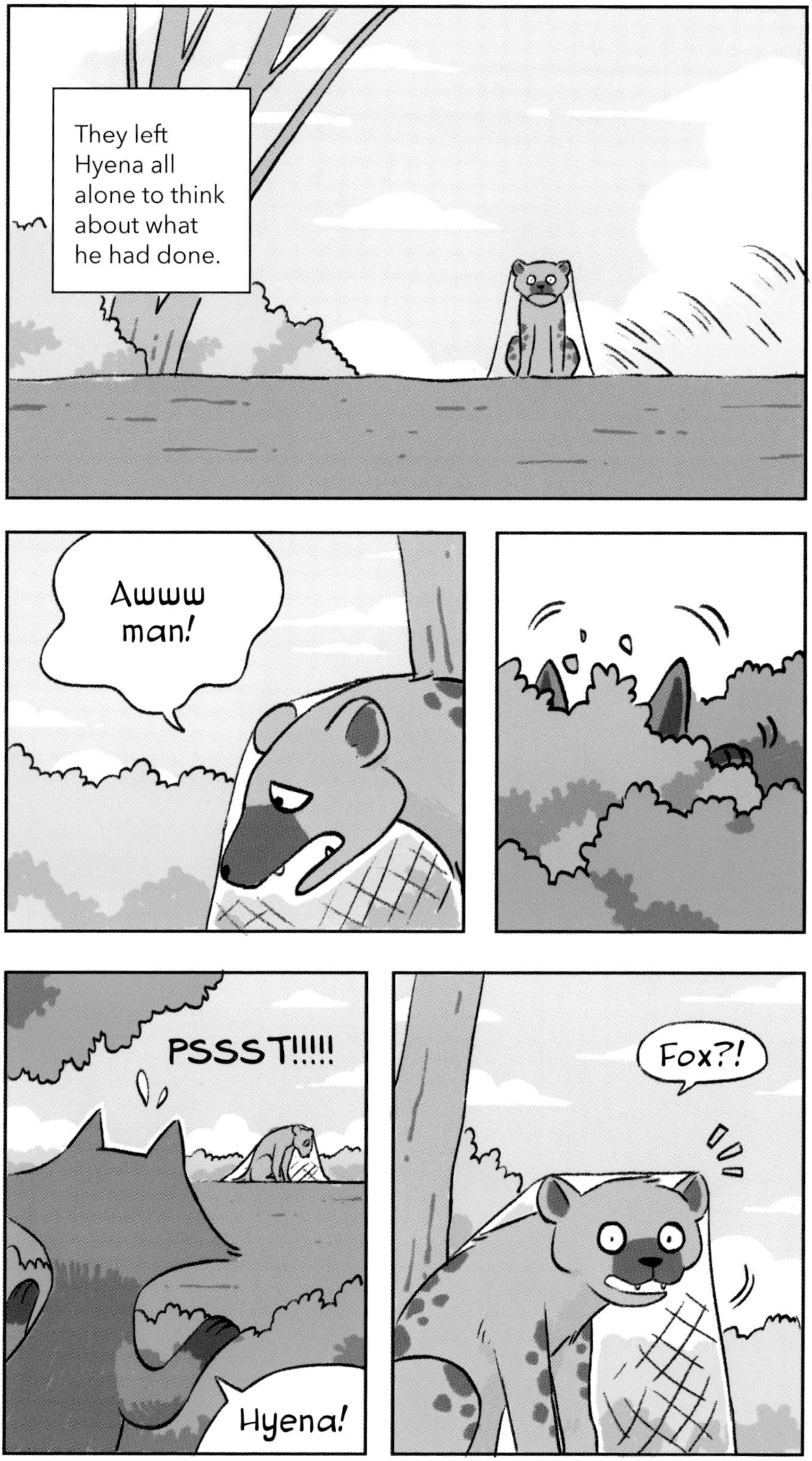
They left Hyena all alone to think about what he had done.
Awww man!
PSSST!!!!!
Hyena!
Fox?!

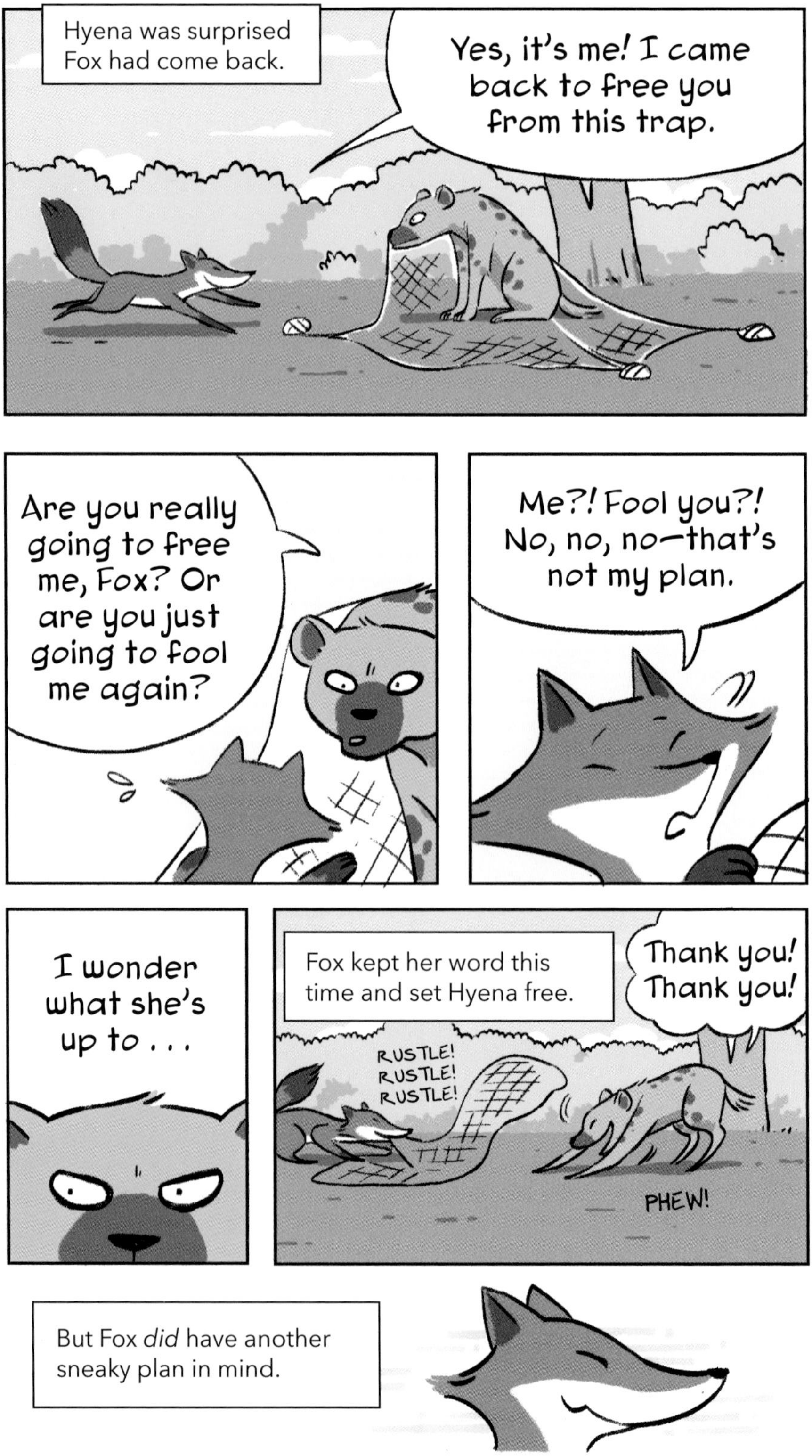
Hyena was surprised Fox had come back.
Yes, it's me! I came back to free you from this trap.
Are you really going to free me, Fox? Or are you just going to fool me again?
Me?! Fool you?! No, no, no—that's not my plan.
I wonder what she's up to . . .
Fox kept her word this time and set Hyena free.
Thank you! Thank you!
RUSTLE! RUSTLE! RUSTLE!
PHEW!
But Fox *did* have another sneaky plan in mind.

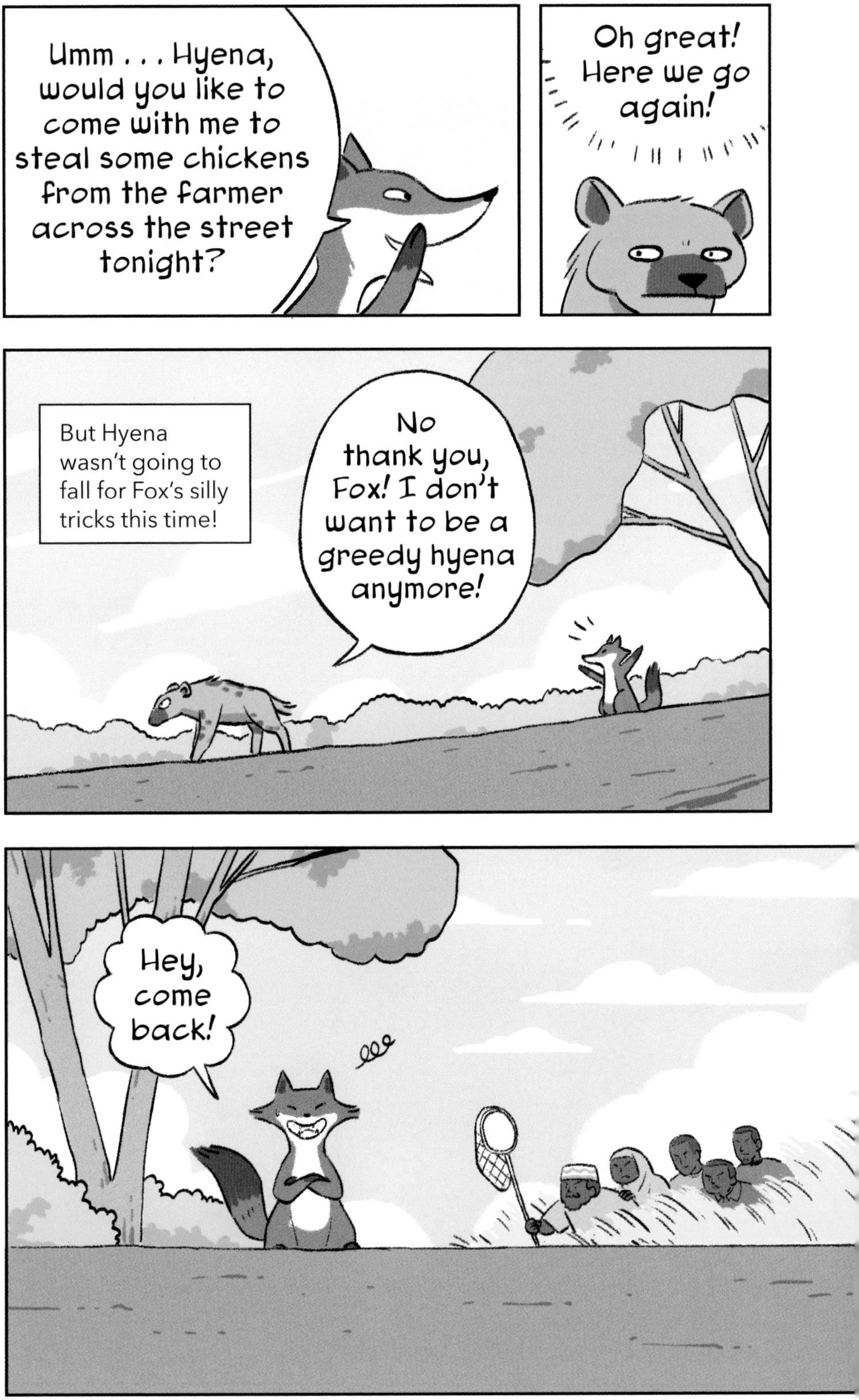
Umm . . . Hyena, would you like to come with me to steal some chickens from the farmer across the street tonight?
Oh great! Here we go again!
But Hyena wasn't going to fall for Fox's silly tricks this time!
No thank you, Fox! I don't want to be a greedy hyena anymore!
Hey, come back!

WRITING PROMPTS

1. The three herdsmen were happy to help their friends, Farmer Ahmed and Asha. Write about a time you helped one of your friends.

2. Do you think Farmer Ahmed and Asha will catch Fox? Write what you think will happen next in the story.

3. Hyena learns his lesson at the end of the story and doesn't listen to Fox. Write about a time you did the wrong thing and learned an important lesson.

DISCUSSION QUESTIONS

1. Asha gets really upset when Fox tries to eat her animals. What is something that makes you really upset?

2. Asha, Farmer Ahmed, and the herdsmen decide to set a trap to stop Fox. What are some other ways they might have kept Fox away from their animals?

3. In the end, Fox tried to get Hyena in trouble again, but Hyena chose to do the right thing. Why is it important to do the right thing?

GLOSSARY

clever (KLEV-uhr)—able to think quickly

fool (FOOL)—to trick

foolish (FOO-lish)—lacking good sense

greedy (GREED-ee)—wanting more than is needed

herdsman (HURDZ-muhn)—someone who raises and keeps farm animals

outsmart (out-SMART)—to trick others by being able to think more quickly

sneaky (SNEEK-ee)—able to move in a secret manner

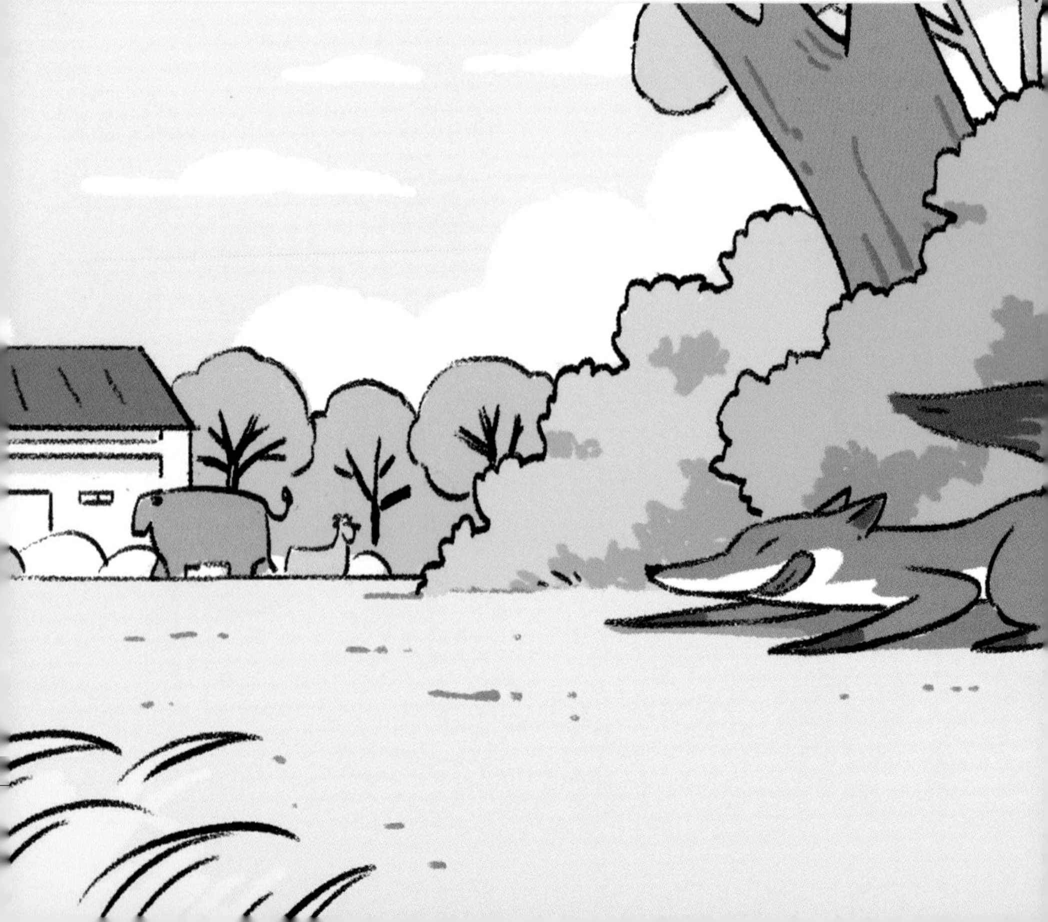

ABOUT THE AUTHOR

As a young girl, Mariam Mohamed grew up watching her father, Osman, write poetry. He inspired her to really tap into her creative side and chase after her dream of becoming a children's author. Now, Mariam has written several children's books, including *Ayeeyo's Golden Rule*, *What I Wish You Knew about My Cousin Ali*, and *Eid Al-Adha*. She is also a teacher who tries her best to encourage her students and help them love writing and reading. Mariam is passionate about baking and spending time with her two daughters Faduma and Kinsi, her husband Sacad, and her mother Yasmin. She lives and works in Minneapolis, Minnesota.

ABOUT THE ILLUSTRATOR

Le Nhat Vu was born in Nha Trang City, a seaside city in Vietnam. While growing up there, he taught himself to draw by studying art documents and the works of other artists. He especially enjoyed reading manga (Japanese comics) and trying to draw the illustrations in his favorite comic books. Today, Nhat Vu works in Ho Chi Minh City, where he loves to watch and play football, read novels, watch movies, and listen to old pop music.

READ ALL THE AMAZING DISCOVER GRAPHICS BOOKS!

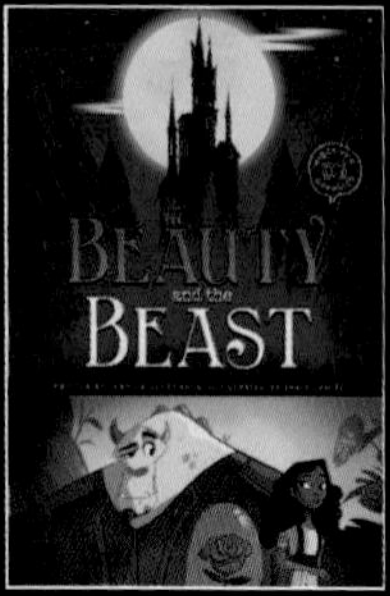
Beauty and the Beast

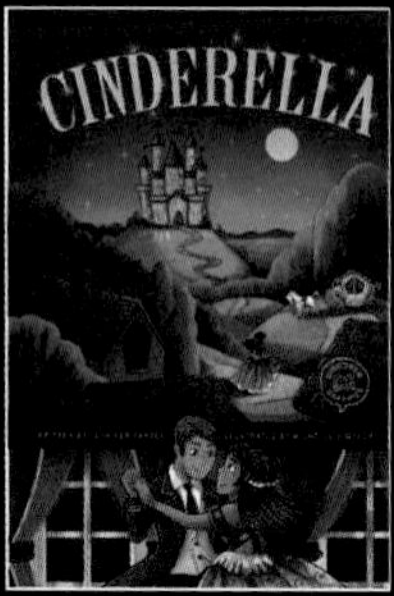
Cinderella

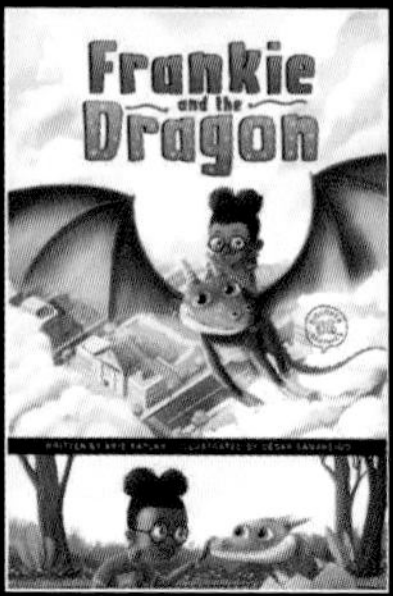
Frankie and the Dragon

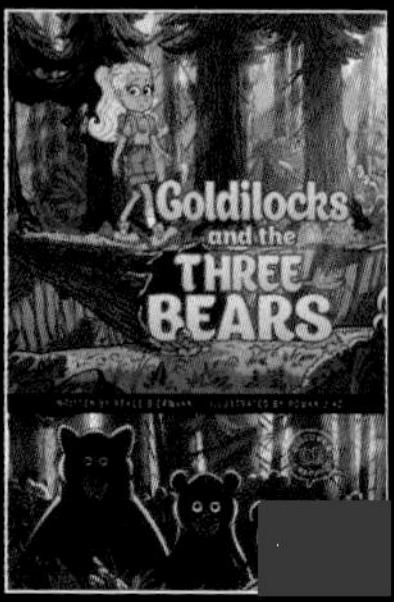
Goldilocks and the Three Bears

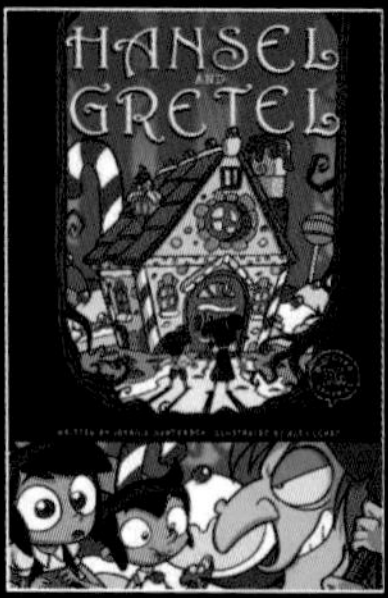
Hansel and Gretel

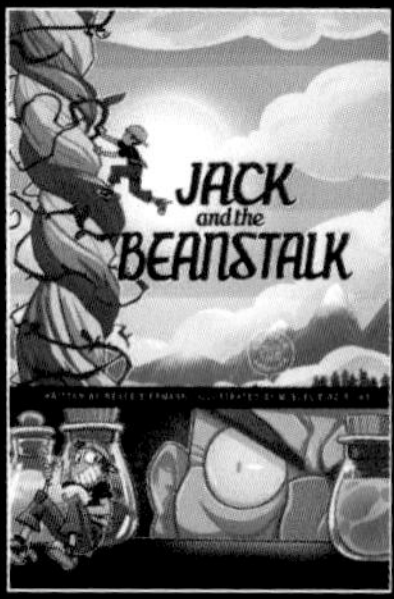
Jack and the Beanstalk

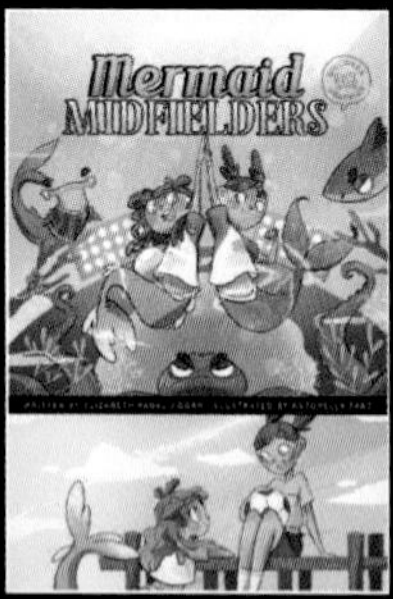
Mermaid Midfielders

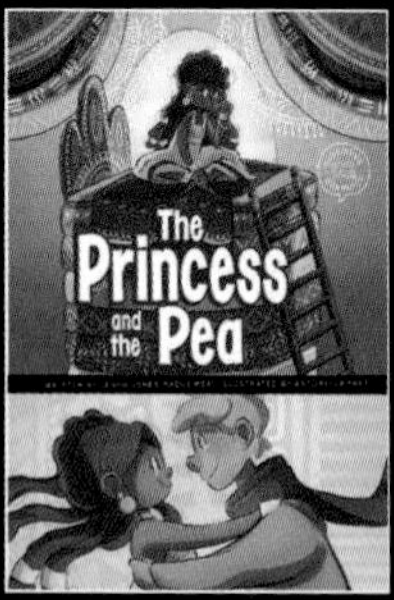
The Princess and the Pea

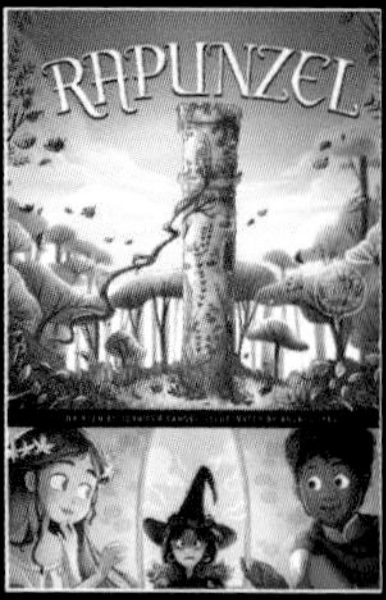
Rapunzel

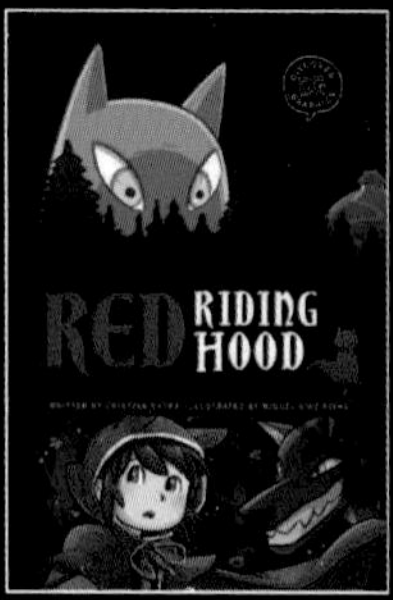
Red Riding Hood

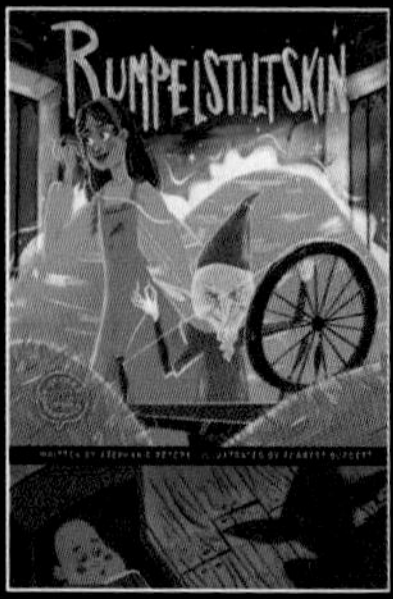
Rumpelstiltskin

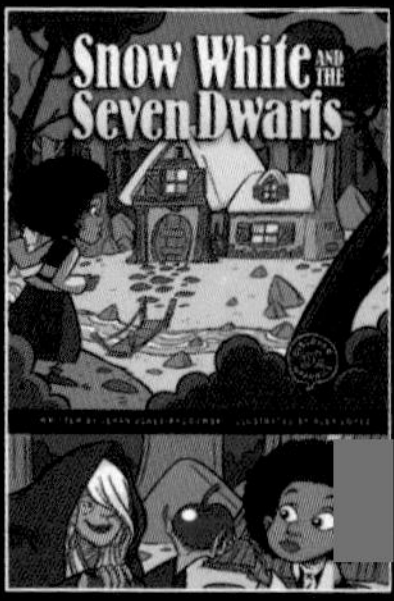
Snow White and the Seven Dwarfs

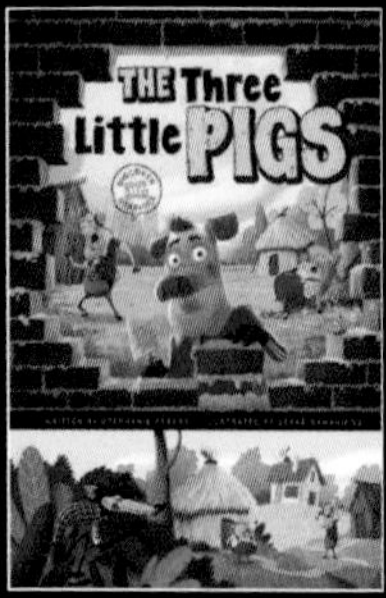
The Three Little Pigs

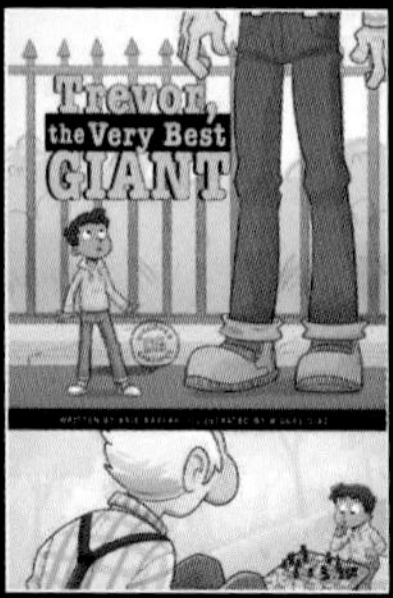
Trevor, the Very Best Giant

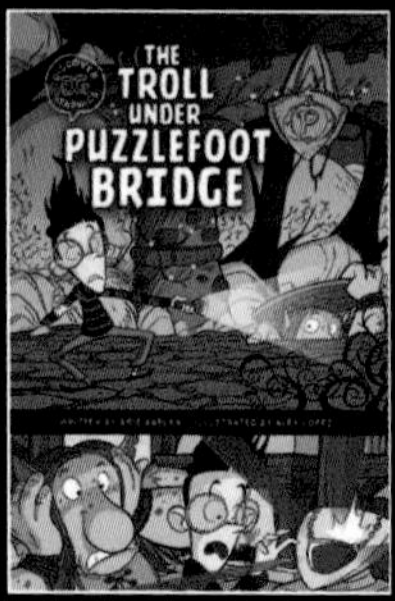
The Troll Under Puzzlefoot Bridge

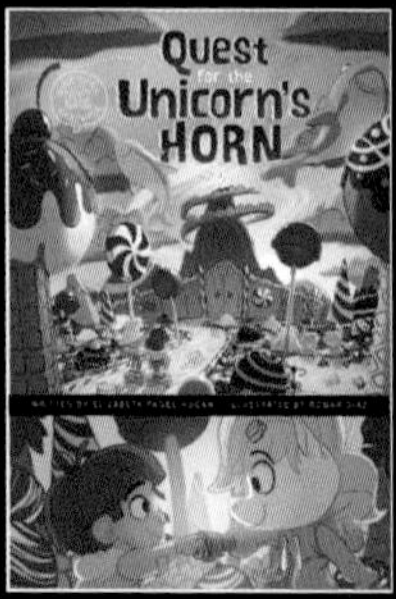
Quest for the Unicorn's Horn